I0652577

Sydney Smith

Peter Plymley's letters and selected essays

Sydney Smith

Peter Plymley's letters and selected essays

ISBN/EAN: 9783337281830

Printed in Europe, USA, Canada, Australia, Japan

Cover: Foto ©Andreas Hilbeck / pixelio.de

More available books at **www.hansebooks.com**

CASSELL'S NATIONAL LIBRARY

PETER PLYMLEY'S LETTERS

AND

SELECTED ESSAYS

BY

SYDNEY SMITH

CASSELL & COMPANY Limited

LONDON PARIS & MELBOURNE

1893

INTRODUCTION.

Sydney Smith, of the same age as Walter Scott, was born at Woodford, in Essex, in the year 1771, and he died of heart disease, aged seventy-four, on the 22nd of February, 1845. His father was a clever man of wandering habits who, when he settled in England, reduced his means by buying, altering, spoiling, and then selling about nineteen different places in England. His mother was of a French family from Languedoc, that had been driven to England by the Revocation of the Edict of Nantes. Sydney Smith's grandfather, upon the mother's side, could speak no English, and he himself ascribed some of his gaiety to the French blood in his veins.

He was one of four sons. His eldest brother Robert —known as Bobus—was sent to Eton, where he joined Canning, Frere, and John Smith, in writing the Eton magazine, the *Microcosm*; and at Cambridge Bobus afterwards was known as a fine Latin scholar. Sydney Smith went first to a school at Southampton, and then to Winchester, where he became captain of the school. Then he was sent for six months to Normandy for a last polish to his French before he went on to New College, Oxford. When he had obtained his fellowship there, his father left him to his own resources. His eldest brother had been trained for the bar, his two younger brothers were sent out to India, and Sydney, against his own wish, yielded to the strong desire of his father that he should take orders as a clergyman. Accordingly, in 1794, he became curate of the small parish of Netherhaven, in Wiltshire. Meat came to Netherhaven only once a week in a butcher's cart from Salisbury, and the curate often dined upon potatoes flavoured with ketchup.

The only educated neighbour was Mr. Hicks Beach, the squire, who at first formally invited the curate to dinner on Sundays, and soon found his wit, sense, and high culture so delightful, that the acquaintance ripened into friendship. After two years in the curacy, Sydney Smith gave it up and went abroad with the squire's son. "When first I went into the Church," he wrote afterwards, "I had a curacy in the middle of Salisbury Plain; the parish was Netherhaven, near Amesbury. The squire of the parish, Mr. Beach, took a fancy to me, and after I had served it two years, he engaged me as tutor to his eldest son, and it was arranged that I and his son should proceed to the University of Weimar in Saxony. We set out, but before reaching our destination Germany was disturbed by war, and, in stress of politics, we put into Edinburgh, where I remained five years."

Young Michael Beach, who had little taste for study, lived with Sydney Smith as his tutor, and found him a wise guide and pleasant friend. When Michael went to the University, his brother William was placed under the same good care. Sydney Smith, about the same time, went to London to be married. His wife's rich brother quarrelled with her for marrying a man who said that his only fortune consisted in six small silver teaspoons. One day after their happy marriage he ran in to his wife and threw them in her lap, saying, " There, Kate, you lucky girl, I give you all my fortune!" The lucky girl had a small fortune of her own which her husband had strictly secured to herself and her children. Mr. Beach recognised the value of Sydney Smith's influence over his son by a wedding gift of £750. In 1802 a daughter was born, and in the same year Sydney Smith joined Francis Jeffrey and other friends, who then maintained credit for Edinburgh as the Modern Athens, in the founding of *The Edinburgh Review*, to which the papers in this volume, added to the Peter Plymley Letters, were contributed. The Rev. Sydney Smith preached sometimes in the Episcopal Church at Edinburgh, and presently had, in addition to William Beach, a son of Mr. Gordon, of Ellon Castle, placed under his care, receiving £400 a year for each of the young men.

In 1803 Sydney Smith left Edinburgh for London, where he wrote busily in *The Edinburgh Review*, but remained poor for many years. His wit brought friends, and the marriage of his eldest brother with Lord Holland's aunt quickened the growth of a strong friendship with Lord Holland. Through the good offices of Lord Holland, Sydney Smith obtained, in 1806, aged thirty-five, the living of Foston-le-Clay, in Yorkshire. In the next year appeared the first letter of Peter Plymley to his brother Abraham on the subject of the Irish Catholics.

These letters fell, we are told, like sparks on a heap of gunpowder. All London, and soon all England, was alive to the sound reason recommended by a lively wit. Sydney Smith lived to be recognised as first

among the social wits, and it was always the chief
praise of his wit that wisdom was the soul of it. Peter
Plymley's letters, and Sydney Smith's articles on the
same subject in *The Edinburgh Review* were the most
powerful aids furnished by the pen to the solution of
the burning question of their time. Lord Murray
called the Plymley letters "after Pascal's letters the
most instructive piece of wisdom in the form of irony
ever written." Worldly wealth came later; but in
wit, wisdom, and kindly helpful cheerfulness, from
youth to age, Sydney Smith's life was rich.

H. M.

LETTERS ON THE SUBJECT OF THE CATHOLICS.

TO
MY BROTHER ABRAHAM,

WHO LIVES IN THE COUNTRY.

BY PETER PLYMLEY.

LETTER I.

DEAR ABRAHAM,—A worthier and better man than
yourself does not exist; but I have always told you,
from the time of our boyhood, that you were a bit of a
goose. Your parochial affairs are governed with exemplary order and regularity; you are as powerful in
the vestry as Mr. Perceval is in the House of Commons,
—and, I must say. with much more reason; nor do I
know any church where the faces and smock-frocks of
the congregation are so clean, or their eyes so uniformly
directed to the preacher. There is another point, upon
which I will do you ample justice; and that is, that
the eyes so directed towards you are wide open; for
the rustic has, in general, good principles, though he
cannot control his animal habits; and, however loud
he may snore, his face is perpetually turned towards
the fountain of orthodoxy.

Having done you this act of justice, I shall proceed, according to our ancient intimacy and familiarity, to explain to you my opinions about the Catholics, and to reply to yours.

In the first place, my sweet Abraham, the Pope is not landed—nor are there any curates sent out after him—nor has he been hid at St. Albans by the Dowager Lady Spencer—nor dined privately at Holland House—nor been seen near Dropmore. If these fears exist (which I do not believe), they exist only in the mind of the Chancellor of the Exchequer; they emanate from his zeal for the Protestant interest; and, though they reflect the highest honour upon the delicate irritability of his faith, must certainly be considered as more ambiguous proofs of the sanity and vigour of his understanding. By this time, however, the best-informed clergy in the neighbourhood of the metropolis are convinced that the rumour is without foundation; and though the Pope is probably hovering about our coast in a fishing-smack, it is most likely he will fall a prey to the vigilance of our cruisers; and it is certain that he has not yet polluted the Protestantism of our soil.

Exactly in the same manner, the story of the wooden gods seized at Charing Cross, by an order from the Foreign Office, turns out to be without the shadow of a foundation; instead of the angels and archangels, mentioned by the informer, nothing was discovered but a wooden image of Lord Mulgrave, going down to Chatham, as a head-piece for the *Spanker* gun-vessel; it was an exact resemblance of his Lordship in his

military uniform; and *therefore* as little like a god as
can well be imagined.

Having set your fears at rest, as to the extent of the
conspiracy formed against the Protestant religion, I
will now come to the argument itself.

You say these men interpret the scriptures in an un-
orthodox manner, and that they eat their god.—Very
likely. All this may seem very important to you, who
live fourteen miles from a market-town, and, from long
residence upon your living, are become a kind of holy
vegetable; and in a theological sense it is highly
important. But I want soldiers and sailors for the
state; I want to make a greater use than I now can do
of a poor country full of men; I want to render the
military service popular among the Irish; to check the
power of France; to make every possible exertion for
the safety of Europe, which in twenty years' time will
be nothing but a mass of French slaves: and then you,
and ten other such boobies as you, call out—"For God's
sake, do not think of raising cavalry and infantry in
Ireland! . . . . They interpret the Epistle to
Timothy in a different manner from what we do! . .
. . They eat a bit of wafer every Sunday, which
they call their God!" . . . . I wish to my soul
they would eat you, and such reasoners as you are.
What! when Turk, Jew, Heretic, Infidel, Catholic,
Protestant, are all combined against this country;
when men of every religious persuasion, and no religious
persuasion; when the population of half the globe is
up in arms against us; are we to stand examining our
generals and armies as a bishop examines a candidate

for holy orders; and to suffer no one to bleed for
England who does not agree with you about the second
of Timothy? You talk about the Catholics! If you
and your brotherhood have been able to persuade the
country into a continuation of this grossest of all
absurdities, you have ten times the power which the
Catholic clergy ever had in their best days. Louis
XIV., when he revoked the Edict of Nantes, never
thought of preventing the Protestants from fighting
his battles; and gained accordingly some of his most
splendid victories by the talents of his Protestant
generals. No power in Europe, but yourselves, has
ever thought for these hundred years past, of asking
whether a bayonet is Catholic, or Presbyterian, or
Lutheran; but whether it is sharp and well-tempered.
A bigot delights in public ridicule; for he begins to
think he is a martyr. I can promise you the full
enjoyment of this pleasure, from one extremity of
Europe to the other.

I am as disgusted with the nonsense of the Roman
Catholic religion as you can be : and no man who
talks such nonsense shall ever tithe the product of the
earth, nor meddle with the ecclesiastical establishment
in any shape; but what have I to do with the specula-
tive nonsense of his theology, when the object is to
elect the mayor of a county town, or to appoint a colonel
of a marching regiment? Will a man discharge the
solemn impertinences of the one office with less zeal, or
shrink from the bloody boldness of the other with
greater timidity, because the blockhead thinks he can
eat angels in muffins and chew a spiritual nature in

the crumpets which he buys from the baker's shop? I
am sorry there should be such impious folly in the
world, but I should be ten times a greater fool than he
is, if I refused, till he had made a solemn protestation
that the crumpet was spiritless and the muffin nothing
but a human muffin, to lead him out against the
enemies of the state. Your whole argument is wrong:
the state has nothing whatever to do with theological
errors which do not violate the common rules of
morality, and militate against the fair power of the
ruler: it leaves all these errors to you, and to such as
you. You have every tenth porker in your parish for
refuting them; and take care that you are vigilant and
logical in the task.

I love the Church as well as you do; but you totally
mistake the nature of an establishment, when you contend that it ought to be connected with the military
and civil career of every individual in the state. It is
quite right that there should be one clergyman to every
parish interpreting the Scriptures after a particular
manner, ruled by a regular hierarchy, and paid with a
rich proportion of haycocks and wheatsheafs. When
I have laid this foundation for a rational religion in
the state—when I have placed ten thousand well-edu-
cated men in different parts of the kingdom to preach
it up, and compelled everybody to pay them, whether
they hear them or not—I have taken such measures as I
know must always procure an immense majority in
favour of the Established Church; but I can go no
further. I cannot set up a civil inquisition, and
say to one, you shall not be a butcher, because you are

not orthodox; and prohibit another from brewing, and
a third from administering the law, and a fourth from
defending the country. If common justice did not
prohibit me from such a conduct, common sense would.
The advantage to be gained by quitting the heresy
would make it shameful to abandon it; and men who
had once left the Church would continue in such a
state of alienation from a point of honour, and transmit
that spirit to their latest posterity. This is just the
effect your disqualifying laws have produced. They
have fed Dr. Rees, and Dr. Kippis; crowded the congregations of the Old Jewry to suffocation: and enabled
every sublapsarian, and superlapsarian, and semi-
pelagian clergyman, to build himself a neat brick
chapel, and live with some distant resemblance to the
state of a gentleman.

You say the King's coronation oath will not allow
him to consent to any relaxation of the Catholic laws.
—Why not relax the Catholic laws as well as the laws
against Protestant dissenters? If one is contrary to
his oath, the other must be so too; for the spirit of the
oath is, to defend the Church establishment, which the
Quaker and the Presbyterian differ from as much or
more than the Catholic; and yet his Majesty has
repealed the Corporation and Test Act in Ireland, and
done more for the Catholics of both kingdoms than
had been done for them since the Reformation. In
1778 the ministers said nothing about the royal conscience; in 1793 no conscience; in 1804 no conscience;
the common feeling of humanity and justice then seem
to have had their fullest influence upon the advisers of

the Crown ; but in 1807—a year, I suppose, eminently
fruitful in moral and religious scruples (as some years
are fruitful in apples, some in hops),—it is contended
by the well-paid John Bowles, and by Mr. Perceval
(who tried to be well paid), that this is now perjury
which we had hitherto called policy and benevolence.
Religious liberty has never made such a stride as under
the reign of his present Majesty; nor is there any
instance in the annals of our history, where so many
infamous and damnable laws have been repealed as
those against the Catholics which have been put an end
to by him ; and then, at the close of this useful policy,
his advisers discover that the very measures of concession and indulgence, or (to use my own language)
the measures of justice, which he has been pursuing
through the whole of his reign, are contrary to the oath
he takes at its commencement! That oath binds his
Majesty not to consent to any measure contrary to the
interest of the Established Church; but who is to
judge of the tendency of each particular measure ?
Not the King alone : it can never be the intention of
this law that the King, who listens to the advice of his
Parliament upon a read bill, should reject it upon the
most important of all measures. Whatever be his own
private judgment of the tendency of any ecclesiastical
bill, he complies most strictly with his oath, if he is
guided in that particular point by the advice of his
Parliament, who may be presumed to understand its
tendency better than the King, or any other individual.
You say, if Parliament had been unanimous in their
opinion of the absolute necessity for Lord Howick's

bill, and the King had thought it pernicious, he would
have been perjured if he had not rejected it.   I say, on
the contrary, his Majesty would have acted in the most
conscientious manner, and have complied most scru-
pulously with his oath, if he had sacrificed his own
opinion to the opinion of the great council of the nation;
because the probability was that such opinion was
better than his own; and upon the same principle, in
common life, you give up your opinion to your physician,
your lawyer, and your builder.

You admit this bill did not compel the King to elect
Catholic officers, but only gave him the option of doing
so if he pleased; but you add, that the King was right
in not trusting such dangerous power to himself or his
successors.   Now you are either to suppose that the
King for the time being has a zeal for the Catholic establishment, or that he has not.   If he has not, where
is the danger of giving such an option? If you suppose
that he may be influenced by such an admiration of the
Catholic religion, why did his present Majesty, in the
year 1804, consent to that bill which empowered the
Crown to station ten thousand Catholic soldiers in any
part of the kingdom, and place them absolutely at the
disposal of the Crown?   If the King of England for
the time being is a good Protestant, there can be no
danger in making the Catholic *eligible* to anything:
if he is not, no power can possibly be so dangerous as
that conveyed by the bill last quoted; to which, in point
of peril, Lord Howick's bill is a mere joke.   But the
real fact is, one bill opened a door to his Majesty's advisers for trick, jobbing, and intrigue; the other did not.

Besides, what folly to talk to me of an oath, which, under all possible circumstances, is to prevent the re-laxation of the Catholic laws! for such a solemn appeal to God sets all conditions and contingencies at defiance. Suppose Bonaparte was to retrieve the only very great blunder he has made, and were to succeed, after repeated trials, in making an impression upon Ireland, do you think we should hear any thing of the impedi-ment of a coronation oath? or would the spirit of this country tolerate for an hour such ministers, and such unheard-of nonsense, if the most distant prospect existed of conciliating the Catholics by every species even of the most abject concession? And yet, if your argument is good for anything, the coronation oath ought to reject, at such a moment, every tendency to conciliation, and to bind Ireland for ever to the crown of France.

I found in your letter the usual remarks about fire, fagot, and bloody Mary. Are you aware, my dear Priest, that there were as many persons put to death for religious opinions under the mild Elizabeth as under the bloody Mary? The reign of the former was, to be sure, ten times as long; but I only mention the fact, merely to show you that something depends upon the age in which men live, as well as on their religious opinions. Three hundred years ago men burnt and hanged each other for these opinions. Time has softened Catholic as well as Protestant: they both re-quired it; though each perceives only his own improve-ment, and is blind to that of the other. We are all the creatures of circumstances. I know not a kinder and better man than yourself; but you, if you had lived in those times, would certainly have roasted your Catholic: and I promise you, if the first exciter of this religious mob had been as powerful then as he is now, you would soon have been elevated to the mitre. I do not go the length of saying that the world has suffered as much from Protestant as from Catholic persecution; far from it: but you should remember the Catholics had all the power, when the idea first started up in the world that there could be two modes of faith; and that it was much more natural they should attempt to crush this diversity of opinion by great and cruel efforts, than that the Protestants should rage against those who differed from them, when the very basis of their system was complete freedom in all spiritual matters.

I cannot extend my letter any further at present, but you shall soon hear from me again. You tell me I am a party man. I hope I shall always be so, when I see my country in the hands of a pert London joker and a second-rate lawyer. Of the first, no other good is known than that he makes pretty Latin verses; the second seems to me to have the head of a country parson and the tongue of an Old Bailey lawyer.

If I could see good measures pursued, I care not a farthing who is in power; but I have a passionate love for common justice, and for common sense, and I abhor and despise every man who builds up his political fortune upon their ruin.

God bless you, reverend Abraham, and defend you from the Pope, and all of us from that administration who seek power by opposing a measure which Burke,

Pitt, and Fox all considered as absolutely necessary to the existence of the country.

LETTER II.

DEAR ABRAHAM,—The Catholic not respect an oath! why not? What upon earth has kept him out of Parliament, or excluded him from all the offices whence he is excluded, but his respect for oaths? There is no law which prohibits a Catholic to sit in Parliament. There could be no such law; because it is impossible to find out what passes in the interior of any man's mind. Suppose it were in contemplation to exclude all men from certain offices who contended for the legality of taking tithes: the only mode of discovering that fervid love of decimation which I know you to possess would be to tender you an oath "against that damnable doctrine, that it is lawful for a spiritual man to take, abstract, appropriate, subduct, or lead away the tenth calf, sheep, lamb, ox, pigeon, duck," &c., &c., &c., and every other animal that ever existed, which of course the lawyers would take care to enumerate. Now this oath I am sure you would rather die than take; and so the Catholic is excluded from Parliament because he will not swear that he disbelieves the leading doctrines of his religion! The Catholic asks you to abolish some oaths which oppress him; your answer is that he does not respect oaths. Then why subject him to the test of oaths? The oaths keep him out of Parliament; why, then, he respects them. Turn which way you will, either your laws are nugatory, or the Catholic is

bound by religious obligations as you are; but no eel
in the well-sanded fist of a cook-maid, upon the eve of
being skinned, ever twisted and writhed as an orthodox
parson does when he is compelled by the gripe of
reason to admit anything in favour of a dissenter.

I will not dispute with you whether the Pope be or
be not the Scarlet Lady of Babylon. I hope it is not
so; because I am afraid it will induce His Majesty's
Chancellor of the Exchequer to introduce several severe
bills against popery, if that is the case; and though he
will have the decency to appoint a previous committee
of inquiry as to the fact, the committee will be garbled,
and the report inflammatory. Leaving this to be
settled as he pleases to settle it, I wish to inform you,
that, previously to the bill last passed in favour of the
Catholics, at the suggestion of Mr. Pitt, and for his
satisfaction, the opinions of six of the most celebrated
of the foreign Catholic universities were taken as to
the right of the Pope to interfere in the temporal concerns of any country. The answer cannot possibly
leave the shadow of a doubt, even in the mind of Baron
Maseres; and Dr. Rennel would be compelled to
admit it, if three Bishops lay dead at the very moment
the question were put to him. To this answer might
be added also the solemn declaration and signature of
all the Catholics in Great Britain.

I should perfectly agree with you, if the Catholics
admitted such a dangerous dispensing power in the
hands of the Pope; but they all deny it, and laugh at
it, and are ready to abjure it in the most decided
manner you can devise. They obey the Pope as the

spiritual head of their Church; but are you really so
foolish as to be imposed upon by mere names? What
matters it the seven-thousandth part of a farthing who
is the spiritual head of any Church? Is not **Mr.**
Wilberforce at the head of the Church of Clapham? Is
not **Dr.** Letsom at the head of the Quaker Church? Is
not the General Assembly at the head of the Church of
Scotland? How is the government disturbed by these
many-headed Churches? or in what way is the power
of the Crown augmented by this almost nominal
dignity?

The King appoints a fast-day once a year, and he
makes the bishops: and if the government would take
half the pains to keep the Catholics out of the arms of
France that it does to widen Temple Bar, or improve
Snow Hill, the King would get into his hands the appointments of the titular Bishops of Ireland. Both
Mr. C——'s sisters enjoy pensions more than sufficient
to place the two greatest dignitaries of the Irish Catholic Church entirely at the disposal of the Crown.
Everybody who knows Ireland knows perfectly well,
that nothing would be easier, with the expenditure of a
little money, than to preserve enough of the ostensible
appointment in the hands of the Pope to satisfy the
scruples of the Catholics, while the real nomination remained with the Crown. But, as I have before said,
the moment the very name of Ireland is mentioned, the
English seem to bid adieu to common feeling, common
prudence, and common sense, and to act with the bar-
barity of tyrants and the fatuity of idiots.

Whatever your opinion may be of the follies of the

Roman Catholic religion, remember they are the follies
of four millions of human beings, increasing rapidly in
numbers, wealth, and intelligence, who, if firmly
united with this country, would set at defiance the
power of France, and if once wrested from their
alliance with England, would in three years render its
existence as an independent nation absolutely impossible. You speak of danger to the Establishment: I request to know when the Establishment was ever so
much in danger as when Hoche was in Bantry Bay, and
whether all the books of Bossuet, or the arts of the
Jesuits, were half so terrible? Mr. Perceval and his
parsons forget all this, in their horror lest twelve or
fourteen old women may be converted to holy water
and Catholic nonsense. They never see that, while
they are saving these venerable ladies from perdition,
Ireland may be lost, England broken down, and the
Protestant Church, with all its deans, prebendaries,
Percevals, and Rennels, be swept into the vortex of
oblivion.

Do not, I beseech you, ever mention to me again the
name of Dr. Duigenan. I have been in every corner
of Ireland, and have studied its present strength and
condition with no common labour. Be assured Ireland does not contain at this moment less than five
millions of people. There were returned in the year
1791 to the hearth tax 701,000 houses, and there is no
kind of question that there were about 50,000 houses
omitted in that return. Taking, however, only the
number returned for the tax, and allowing the average
of six to a house (a very small average for a potato-fed

people), this brings the population to 4,200,000 people
in the year 1791 : and it can be shown from the
clearest evidence (and Mr. Newenham in his book
shows it), that Ireland for the last fifty years has increased in its population at the rate of 50 or 60,000
per annum; which leaves the present population of
Ireland at about five millions, after every possible
deduction for *existing circumstances, just and necessary
wars, monstrous and unnatural rebellions*, and all
other sources of human destruction. Of this population,
two out of ten are Protestants; and the half of the
Protestant population are Dissenters, and as inimical
to the Church as the Catholics themselves. In this
state of things thumbscrews and whipping—admirable
engines of policy as they must be considered to be—
will not ultimately avail. The Catholics will hang
over you; they will watch for the moment, and compel you hereafter to give them ten times as much,
against your will. as they would now be contented
with, if it were voluntarily surrendered. Remember
what happened in the American war, when Ireland
compelled you to give her everything she asked, and
to renounce, in the most explicit manner, your claim
of Sovereignty over her. God Almighty grant the
folly of these present men may not bring on such
another crisis of public affairs !

What are your dangers which threaten the Establish-
blishment ?—Reduce this declamation to a point, and
let us understand what you mean. The most ample
allowance does not calculate that there would be more
than twenty members who were Roman Catholics in

·one house, and ten in the other, if the Catholic emancipation were carried into effect. Do you mean that
these thirty members would bring in a bill to take
·away the tithes from the Protestant, and to pay them
to the Catholic clergy? Do you mean that a Catholic
general would march his army into the House of Commons, and purge it of Mr. Perceval and Dr. Duigenan?
or, that the theological writers would become all of
a sudden more acute or more learned, if the present
civil incapacities were removed? Do you fear for
your tithes, or your doctrines, or your person, or the
English Constitution? Every fear, taken separately,
is so glaringly absurd, that no man has the folly or
the boldness to state it. Every one conceals his
ignorance, or his baseness, in a stupid general panic,
which, when called on, he is utterly incapable of
explaining. Whatever you think of the Catholics,
there they are—you cannot get rid of them; your
alternative is to give them a lawful place for stating
their grievances, or an unlawful one: if you do not
admit them to the House of Commons, they will hold
their parliament in Potatoe Place, Dublin, and be ten
times as violent and inflammatory as they would be in
Westminster. Nothing would give me such an idea
of security as to see twenty or thirty Catholic gentlemen in Parliament, looked upon by all the Catholics
as the fair and proper organ of their party. I should
have thought it the height of good fortune that such a
wish existed on their part, and the very essence of
madness and ignorance to reject it. Can you murder
the Catholics? Can you neglect them? They are

too numerous for both these expedients. What remains to be done is obvious to every human being—
but to that man who, instead of being a Methodist
preacher, is, for the curse of us and our children, and
for the ruin of Troy and the misery of good old Priam
and his sons, become a legislator and a politician.

A distinction, I perceive, is taken by one of the
most feeble noblemen in Great Britain, between persecution and the deprivation of political power; whereas,
there is no more distinction between these two things
than there is between him who makes the distinction
and a booby. If I strip off the relic-covered jacket
of a Catholic, and give him twenty stripes . . . . I persecute; if I say, Everybody in the town where you
live shall be a candidate for lucrative and honourable
offices, but you, who are a Catholic . . . . I do not
persecute! What barbarous nonsense is this! as if
degradation was not as great an evil as bodily pain or
as severe poverty: as if I could not be as great a
tyrant by saying, You shall not enjoy—as by saying,
You shall suffer. The English, I believe, are as
truly religious as any nation in Europe; I know no
greater blessing; but it carries with it this evil in its
train, that any villain who will bawl out, "The Church
is in danger!" may get a place and a good pension;
and that any administration who will do the same
thing may bring a set of men into power who, at a
moment of stationary and passive piety, would be
hooted by the very boys in the streets. But it is not
all religion; it is, in great part, the narrow and exclusive spirit which delights to keep the common

blessings of sun and air and freedom from other
human beings. "Your religion has always been degraded; you are in the dust, and I will take care you
never rise again. I should enjoy less the possession
of an earthly good by every additional person to whom
it was extended." You may not be aware of it yourself, most reverend Abraham, but you deny their freedom to the Catholics upon the same principle that
Sarah your wife refuses to give the receipt for a ham
or a gooseberry dumpling: she values her receipts,
not because they secure to her a certain flavour, but
because they remind her that her neighbours want it:—
a feeling laughable in a priestess, shameful in a priest;
venial when it withholds the blessings of a ham, tyrannical and execrable when it narrows the boon of
religious freedom.

You spend a great deal of ink about the character of
the present prime minister. Grant you all that you
write—I say, I fear he will ruin Ireland, and pursue
a line of policy destructive to the true interest of his
country : and then you tell me, he is faithful to Mrs.
Perceval, and kind to the Master Percevals! These
are, undoubtedly, the first qualifications to be looked
to in a time of the most serious public danger; but
somehow or another (if public and private virtues
must always be incompatible), I should prefer that he
destroyed the domestic happiness of Wood or Cockell,
owed for the veal of the preceding year, whipped his
boys, and saved his country.

The late administration did not do right; they did
not build their measures upon the solid basis of facts.

They should have caused several Catholics to have
been dissected after death by surgeons of either religion;
and the report to have been published with accompany-
ing plates. If the viscera, and other organs of life,
had been found to be the same as in Protestant bodies;
if the provisions of nerves, arteries, cerebrum, and
cerebellum, had been the same as we are provided
with, or as the Dissenters are now known to possess;
then, indeed, they might have met Mr. Perceval upon
a proud eminence, and convinced the country at large
of the strong probability that the Catholics are really
human creatures, endowed with the feelings of men,
and entitled to all their rights. But instead of this
wise and prudent measure, Lord Howick, with his
usual precipitation, brings forward a bill in their
favour, without offering the slightest proof to the
country that they were anything more than horses and
oxen. The person who shows the lama at the corner
of Piccadilly has the precaution to write up—*Allowed
by Sir Joseph Banks to be a real quadruped*, so his
Lordship might have said—*Allowed by the bench of
Bishops to be real human creatures*. . . . I could write
you twenty letters upon this subject; but I am tired,
and so I suppose are you. Our friendship is now of
forty years' standing; you know me to be a truly
religious man; but I shudder to see religion treated
like a cockade, or a pint of beer, and made the instrument of a party. I love the king, but I love the
people as well as the king; and if I am sorry to see his
old age molested, I am much more sorry to see four
millions of Catholics baffled in their just expectations.

If I love Lord Grenville, and Lord Howick, it is
because they love their country; if I abhor . . . .
it is because I know there is but one man among them
who is not laughing at the enormous folly and credulity
of the country, and that he is an ignorant and mischievous bigot. As for the light and frivolous jester,
of whom it is your misfortune to think so highly,
learn, my dear Abraham, that this political Killigrew,
just before the breaking-up of the last administration,
was in actual treaty with them for a place; and if they
had survived twenty-four hours longer, he would have
been now declaiming against the cry of No Popery!
instead of inflaming it. With this practical comment
on the baseness of human nature, I bid you adieu!

LETTER III.

ALL that I have so often told you, Mr. Abraham
Plymley, is now come to pass. The Scythians, in
whom you and the neighbouring country gentleman
placed such confidence, are smitten hip and thigh; their
Beningsen put to open shame; their magazines of
train oil intercepted, and we are waking from our disgraceful drunkenness to all the horrors of Mr. Perceval
and Mr Canning. . . . We shall now see if a nation is
to be saved by school-boy jokes and doggrel rhymes,
by affronting petulance, and by the tones and gesticu-
lations of Mr. Pitt. But these are not all the auxiliaries on
which we have to depend; to these his colleague will add
the strictest attention to the smaller parts of ecclesiastical government, to hassocks, to psalters, and to sur-

plices; in the last agonies of England, he will bring
in a bill to regulate Easter-offerings : and he will ad-
just the stipends of curates, when the flag of France is
unfurled on the hills of Kent. Whatever can be done
by very mistaken notions of the piety of a Christian,
and by a very wretched imitation of the eloquence of
Mr. Pitt, will be done by these two gentlemen. After
all, if they both really were what they both either wish
to be, or wish to be thought; if the one were an enlightened Christian who drew from the Gospel the
toleration, the charity, and the sweetness which it contains; and if the other really possessed any portion of
the great understanding of his Nisus who guarded him
from the weapons of the Whigs, I should still doubt if
they could save us. But I am sure we are not to be
saved by religious hatred, and by religious trifling ; by
any psalmody, however sweet; or by any persecution, however sharp; I am certain the sounds of Mr.
Pitt's voice, and the measure of his tones, and the
movement of his arms, will do nothing for us; when
these tones and movements, and voice brings us always
declamation without sense or knowledge, and ridicule
without good humour or conciliation. Oh, Mr.
Plymley, this never will do. Mrs. Abraham Plymley,
my sister, will be led away captive by an amorous
Gaul; and Joel Plymley your firstborn, will be a
French drummer.

   Out of sight, out of mind, seems to be a proverb
which applies to enemies as well as friends Because
the French army was no longer seen from the cliffs of
Dover; because the sound of cannon was no longer

heard by the debauched London bathers on the Sussex
coast; because the *Morning Post* no longer fixed the
invasion sometimes for Monday, sometimes for Tuesday,
sometimes (positively for the last time of invading) on
Saturday; because all these causes of terror were suspended, you conceived the power of Bonaparte to be at
an end, and were setting off for Paris with Lord
Hawkesbury the conqueror.   This is precisely the
method in which the English have acted during the whole
of the revolutionary war.   If Austria or Prussia armed,
doctors of divinity immediately printed those passages
out of Habakkuk, in which the destruction of the
Usurper by General Mack, and the Duke of Brunswick,
are so clearly predicted.   If Bonaparte halted, there
was a mutiny or a dysentery.   If any one of his generals
were eaten up by the light troops of Russia, and
picked (as their manner is) to the bone, the sanguine
spirit of this country displayed itself in all its glory.
What scenes of infamy did the Society for the Sup-
pression of Vice lay open to our astonished eyes!
tradesmen's daughters dancing, pots of beer carried out
between the first and second lesson, and dark and distant rumours of indecent prints.   Clouds of Mr. Canning's cousins arrived by the waggon; all the contractors left their cards with Mr. Rose; and every plunderer of the public crawled out of his hole, like slugs,
and grubs, and worms after a shower of rain.

　　If my voice could have been heard at the late changes,
I should have said, " Gently, patience, stop a little; the
time is not yet come; the mud of Poland will harden,
and the bowels of the French grenadiers will recover

their tone. When honesty, good sense, and liberality have extricated you out of your present embarrassment, then dismiss them as a matter of course; but you cannot spare them just now; don't be in too great a hurry, or there will be no monarch to flatter, and no country to pillage; only submit for a little time to be respected abroad, overlook the painful absence of the tax-gatherer for a few years, bear up nobly under the increase of freedom and of liberal policy for a little time, and I promise you, at the expiration of that period, you shall be plundered, insulted, disgraced, and restrained to your heart's content. Do not imagine I have any intention of putting servility and canting hypocrisy permanently out of place, or of filling up with courage and sense those offices which naturally devolve upon decorous imbecility and flexible cunning : give us only a little time to keep off the hussars of France, and then the jobbers and jesters shall return to their birthright, and public virtue be called by its own name of fanaticism." Such is the advice I would have offered to my infatuated countrymen : but it rained very hard in November, Brother Abraham, and the bowels of our enemies were loosened, and we put our trust in white fluxes and wet mud; and there is nothing now to oppose to the conqueror of the world but a small table wit, and the sallow Surveyor of the Meltings.

You ask me, if I think it possible for this country to survive the recent misfortunes of Europe?—I answer you, without the slightest degree of hesitation : that if Bonaparte lives, and a great deal is not immediately done for the conciliation of the Catholics, it does seem to me absolutely impossible but that we must perish; and take this with you, that we shall perish without exciting the slightest feeling of present or future compassion, but fall amidst the hootings and revilings of Europe, as a nation of blockheads, Methodists, and old women. If there were any great scenery, any heroic feelings, any blaze of ancient virtue, any exalted death, any termination of England that would be ever remembered, ever honoured in that western world, where liberty is now retiring, conquest would be more tolerable, and ruin more sweet; but it is doubly miserable to become slaves abroad, because we would be tyrants at home; to persecute, when we are contending against persecution; and to perish, because we have raised up worse enemies within, from our own bigotry, than we are exposed to without, from the unprincipled ambition of France. It is indeed, a most silly and affecting spectacle to rage at such a moment against our own kindred and our own blood; to tell them they cannot be honourable in war, because they are conscientious in religion; to stipulate (at the very moment when we should 'buy their hearts and swords at any price (that they must hold up the right hand in prayer, and not the left; and adore one common God, by turning to the east rather than to the west.

What is it the Catholics ask of you? Do not exclude us from the honours and emoluments of the state because we worship God in one way, and you worship Him in another. In a period of the deepest peace, and the fattest prosperity, this would be a fair request; it

should be granted, if Lord Hawkesbury had reached
Paris, if Mr. Canning's interpreter had threatened the
Senate in an opening speech, or Mr. Perceval explained
to them the improvements he meant to introduce into
the Catholic religion ; but to deny the Irish this justice
now, in the present state of Europe, and in the summer
months, just as the season for destroying kingdoms is
coming on, is (beloved Abraham), whatever you may
think of it, little short of positive insanity.

Here is a frigate attacked by a corsair of immense
strength and size, rigging cut, masts in danger of coming by the board, four foot water in the hold, men
dropping off very fast ; in this dreadful situation how
do you think the Captain acts (whose name shall be
Perceval) ? He calls all hands upon deck ; talks to
them of King, country, glory, sweethearts, gin, French
prison, wooden shoes, Old England, and hearts of oak ;
they give three cheers, rush to their guns, and, after a
tremendous conflict, succeed in beating off the enemy.
Not a syllable of all this ; this is not the manner in
which the honourable Commander goes to work : the
first thing he does is to secure twenty or thirty of his
prime sailors who happen to be Catholics, to clap them
in irons, and set over them a guard of as many Protestants ; having taken this admirable method of defending himself against his infidel opponents, he goes upon
deck, reminds the sailors in a very bitter harangue, that
they are of different religions ; exhorts the Episcopal
gunner not to trust to the Presbyterian quartermaster ;
issues positive orders that the Catholics should be fired
at upon the first appearance of discontent ; rushes

B—46

through blood and brains, examining his men in the Catechism and thirty-nine Articles, and positively forbids every one to sponge or ram who has not taken the Sacrament according to the Church of England. Was it right to take out a captain made of excellent British stuff, and to put in such a man as this? Is not he more like a parson, or a talking lawyer, than a thorough-bred seaman? And built as she is of heart of oak, and admirably manned, is it possible, with such a captain, to save this ship from going to the bottom?

You have an argument, I perceive, in common with many others, against the Catholics, that their demands complied with would only lead to further exactions, and that it is better to resist them now, before anything is conceded, than hereafter, when it is found that all concessions are in vain. I wish the Chancellor of the Exchequer, who uses this reasoning to exclude others from their just rights, had tried its efficacy, not by his understanding, but by (what are full of much better things) his pockets. Suppose the person to whom he applied for the meltings had withstood every plea of wife and fourteen children, no business, and good character, and refused him this paltry little office because he might hereafter attempt to get hold of the revenues of the Duchy of Lancaster for life? would not Mr. Perceval have contended eagerly against the injustice of refusing moderate requests, because immoderate ones may hereafter be made? Would he not have said, and said truly, Leave such exorbitant attempts as these to the general indignation of the Commons, who will take care to defeat them when they do occur; but do not refuse me the Irons and the Meltings now, because I may totally lose sight of all moderation hereafter? Leave hereafter to the spirit and the wisdom of hereafter; and do not be niggardly now from the apprehension that men as wise as you should be profuse in times to come.

You forget, Brother Abraham, that is a vast art, where quarrels cannot be avoided, to turn public opinion in your favour and to the prejudice of your enemy; a vast privilege to feel that you are in the right, and to make him feel that he is in the wrong : a privilege which makes you more than a man, and your antagonist less; and often secures victory by convincing him who contends that he must submit to injustice if he submits to defeat. Open every rank in the army and the navy to the Catholic; let him purchase at the same price as the Protestant (if either Catholic or Protestant can purchase such refined pleasures) the privilege of hearing Lord Castlereagh speak for three hours; keep his clergy from starving, soften some of the most odious powers of the tithing-man, and you will for ever lay this formidable question to rest. But if I am wrong, and you must quarrel at last, quarrel upon just rather than unjust grounds; divide the Catholic and unite the Protestant; be just, and your own exertions will be more formidable and their exertions less formidable; be just, and you will take away from their party all the best and wisest understandings of both persuasions, and knit them firmly to your own cause. " Thrice is he armed who has his quarrel just ; " and ten times as much may he

be taxed. In the beginning of any war, however destitute of common sense, every mob will roar, and every
Lord of the Bedchamber address ; but if you are
engaged in a war that is to last for years, and to
require important sacrifices, take care to make the
justice of your case so clear and so obvious that it cannot be mistaken by the most illiterate country gentleman who rides the earth. Nothing, in fact, can be so
grossly absurd as the argument which says I will
deny justice to you now, because I suspect future injustice from you. At this rate, you may lock a man
up in your stable, and refuse to let him out, because
you suspect that he has an intention, at some future
period, of robbing your hen-roost. You may horse-
whip him at Lady Day, because you believe he will
affront you at Midsummer. You may commit a greater
evil, to guard against a less which is merely contingent,
and may never happen. You may do what you have
done a century ago in Ireland, make the Catholics
worse than Helots, because you suspected that they
might hereafter aspire to be more than fellow citizens ;
rendering their sufferings certain from your jealousy,
while yours were only doubtful from their ambition ;
an ambition sure to be excited by the very measures
which were taken to prevent it.

The physical strength of the Catholics will not be
greater because you give them a share of political
power. You may by these means turn rebels into
friends ; but I do not see how you make rebels more
formidable. If they taste of the honey of lawful
power, they will love the hive from whence they

procure it; if they will struggle with us like men in the same state for civil influence, we are safe. All that I dread is the physical strength of four millions of men combined with an invading French army. If you are to quarrel at last with this enormous population, still put it off as long as you can; you must gain, and cannot lose, by the delay. The state of Europe cannot be worse; the conviction which the Catholics entertain of your tyranny and injustice cannot be more alarming, nor the opinions of your own people more divided. Time, which produces such effect upon brass and marble, may inspire one Minister with modesty and another with compassion; every circumstance may be better; some certainly will be so, none can be worse; and after all the evil may never happen.

You have got hold, I perceive, of all the vulgar English stories respecting the hereditary transmission of forfeited property, and seriously believe that every Catholic beggar wears the terriers of his father's land next his skin, and is only waiting for better times to cut the throat of the Protestant possessor, and get drunk in the hall of his ancestors. There is one irresistible answer to this mistake, and that is, that the forfeited lands are purchased indiscriminately by Catholic and Protestant, and that the Catholic purchaser never objects to such a title. Now the land so purchased by a Catholic is either his own family estate, or it is not. If it is, you suppose him so desirous of coming into possession that he resorts to the double method of rebellion and purchase; if it is not his own family estate of which he becomes the purchaser, you suppose him

first to purchase, then to rebel, in order to defeat the
purchase. These things may happen in Ireland, but it
is totally impossible they can happen anywhere else.
In fact, what land can any man of any sect purchase in
Ireland, but forfeited property? In all other oppressed
countries which I have ever heard of, the rapacity of
the conqueror was bounded by the territorial limits in
which the objects of his avarice were contained; but
Ireland has been actually confiscated twice over, as a
cat is twice killed by a wicked parish boy.

I admit there is a vast luxury in selecting a particular set of Christians, and in worrying them as a
boy worries a puppy dog; it is an amusement in which
all the young English are brought up from their
earliest days. I like the idea of saying to men who
use a different hassock from me, that till they change
their hassock they shall never be Colonels, Aldermen,
or Parliament-men. While I am gratifying my
personal insolence respecting religious forms, I fondle
myself into an idea that I am religious, and that I am
doing my duty in the most exemplary, as I certainly
am in the most easy, way. But then, my good
Abraham, this sport, admirable as it is, is become,
with respect to the Catholics, a little dangerous; and
if we are not extremely careful in taking the amusement, we shall tumble into the holy water and be
drowned. As it seems necessary to your idea of an
established church to have somebody to worry and
torment, suppose we were to select for this purpose
William Wilberforce, Esq., and the patent Christians
of Clapham. We shall by this expedient enjoy the

same opportunity for cruelty and injustice, without being exposed to the same risks : we will compel them to abjure vital clergymen by a public test, to deny that the said William Wilberforce has any power of working miracles, touching for barrenness or any other infirmity, or that he is endowed with any preternatural gift whatever. We will swear them to the doctrine of good works, compel them to preach common sense, and to hear it ; to frequent Bishops, Deans, and other High Churchmen ; and to appear, once in the quarter at the least, at some melodrame, opera, pantomime, or other light scenical representation ; in short, we will gratify the love of insolence and power ; we will enjoy the old orthodox sport of witnessing the impotent anger of men compelled to submit to civil degradation, or to sacrifice their notions of truth to ours. And all this we may do without the slightest risk, because their numbers are, as yet, not very considerable. Cruelty and injustice must, of course, exist ; but why connect them with danger ? Why torture a bulldog when you can get a frog or a rabbit ? I am sure my proposal will meet with the most universal approbation. Do not be apprehensive of any opposition from ministers. If it is a case of hatred, we are sure that one man will defend it by the Gospel ; if it abridges human freedom, we know that another will find precedents for it in the Revolution.

In the name of Heaven, what are we to gain by suffering Ireland to be rode by that faction which now predominates over it ? Why are we to endanger our own Church and State, not for 500,000 Episcopalians,

but for ten or twelve great Orange families, who have
been sucking the blood of that country for these
hundred years last past? and the folly of the Orangemen in playing this game themselves, is almost as
absurd as ours in playing it for them. They ought to
have the sense to see that their business now is to
keep quietly the lands and beeves of which the fathers
of the Catholics were robbed in days of yore; they
must give to their descendants the sop of political
power: by contending with them for names, they will
lose realities, and be compelled to beg their potatoes in
a foreign land, abhorred equally by the English, who
have witnessed their oppression, and by the Catholic
Irish, who have smarted under them.

LETTER IV.

THEN comes Mr. Isaac Hawkins Brown (the gentleman who danced so badly at the Court of Naples), and
asks if it is not an anomaly to educate men in another
religion than your own. It certainly is our duty to
get rid of error, and, above all, of religious error; but
this is not to be done *per saltum*, or the measure will
miscarry, like the Queen. It may be very easy to
dance away the royal embryo of a great kingdom; but
Mr. Hawkins Brown must look before he leaps, when
his object is to crush an opposite sect in religion; false
steps aid the one effect as much as they are fatal to
the other: it will require not only the lapse of Mr.
Hawkins Brown, but the lapse of centuries, before the
absurdities of the Catholic religion are laughed at as

much as they deserve to be; but surely, in the meantime, the Catholic religion is better than none; four millions of Catholics are better than four millions of wild beasts; two hundred priests educated by our own government are better than the same number educated by the man who means to destroy us.

The whole sum now appropriated by Government to the religious education of four millions of Christians is £13,000; a sum about one hundred times as large being appropriated in the same country to about one-eighth part of this number of Protestants. When it was proposed to raise this grant from £8,000 to £13,000, its present amount, this sum was objected to by that most indulgent of Christians, Mr. Spencer Perceval, as enormous; he himself having secured for his own eating and drinking, and the eating and drinking of the Master and Miss Percevals, the reversionary sum of £21,000 a year of the public money, and having just failed in a desperate and rapacious attempt to secure to himself for life the revenues of the Duchy of Lancaster: and the best of it is, that this minister, after abusing his predecessors for their impious bounty to the Catholics, has found himself compelled, from the apprehension of immediate danger, to grant the sum in question, thus dissolving his pearl in vinegar, and destroying all the value of the gift by the virulence and reluctance with which it was granted.

I hear from some persons in Parliament, and from others in the sixpenny societies for debate, a great deal about unalterable laws passed at the Revolution,

When I hear any man talk of an unalterable law, the
only effect it produces upon me is to convince me that
he is an unalterable fool. A law passed when there
was Germany, Spain, Russia, Sweden, Holland, Por-
tugal, and Turkey; when there was a disputed
succession; when four or five hundred acres were
won and lost after ten years' hard fighting; when
armies were commanded by the sons of kings, and
campaigns passed in an interchange of civil letters
and ripe fruit; and for these laws, when the whole
state of the world is completely changed, we are now,
according to my Lord Hawkesbury, to hold ourselves
ready to perish. It is no mean misfortune, in times
like these, to be forced to say anything about such
men as Lord Hawkesbury, and to be reminded that we
are governed by them, but as I am driven to it, I
must take the liberty of observing that the wisdom and
liberality of my Lord Hawkesbury are of that complexion which always shrinks from the present exercise of these virtues by praising the splendid examples
of them in ages past. If he had lived at such periods,
he would have opposed the Revolution by praising the
Reformation, and the Reformation by speaking hand-
somely of the Crusades. He gratifies his natural
antipathy to great and courageous measures by playing
off the wisdom and courage which have ceased to
influence human affairs against that wisdom and
courage which living men would employ for present
happiness. Besides, it happens unfortunately for the
Warden of the Cinque Ports, that to the principal incapacities under which the Irish suffer, they were

subjected after that great and glorious revolution, to which we are indebted for so many blessings, and his Lordship for the termination of so many periods. The Catholics were not excluded from the Irish House of Commons, or military commands, before the 3rd and 4th of William and Mary, and the 1st and 2nd of Queen Anne.

If the great mass of the people, environed as they are on every side with Jenkinsons, Percevals, Melvilles, and other perils, were to pray for divine illumination and aid, what more could Providence in its mercy do than send them the example of Scotland? For what a length of years was it attempted to compel the Scotch to change their religion: horse, foot, artillery, and armed Prebendaries, were sent out after the Presbyterian parsons and their congregations. The Percevals of those days called for blood: this call is never made in vain, and blood was shed; but, to the astonishment and horror of the Percevals of those days, they could not introduce the book of Common Prayer, nor prevent that metaphysical people from going to heaven their true way, instead of our true way. With a little oatmeal for food, and a little sulphur for friction, allaying cutaneous irritation with the one hand, and holding his Calvinistical creed in the other, Sawney ran away to his flinty hills, sung his psalm out of tune his own way, and listened to his sermon of two hours long, amid the rough and imposing melancholy of the tallest thistles. But Sawney brought up his unbreeched offspring in a cordial hatred of his oppressors; and Scotland was as much a part of the

weakness of England then as Ireland is at this moment.
The true and the only remedy was applied; the
Scotch were suffered to worship God after their own
tiresome manner, without pain, penalty, or privation.
No lightning descended from heaven : the country was
not ruined; the world is not yet come to an end ; the
dignitaries who foretold all these consequences are
utterly forgotten, and Scotland has ever since been an
increasing source of strength to Great Britain. In
the six hundredth year of our empire over Ireland we
are making laws to transport a man if he is found out
of his house after eight o'clock at night. That this is
necessary I know too well; but tell me why it is
necessary. It is not necessary in Greece, where the
Turks are masters.

Are you aware that there is at this moment a
universal clamour throughout the whole of Ireland
against the Union? It is now one month since I returned from that country ; I have never seen so extraordinary, so alarming, and so rapid a change in the
sentiments of any people. Those who disliked the
Union before are quite furious against it now; those
who doubted doubt no more; those who were friendly
to it have exchanged that friendship for the most rooted
aversion; in the midst of all this (which is by far the
most alarming symptom), there is the strongest disposition on the part of the northern Dissenters to unite with
the Catholics, irritated by the faithless injustice with
which they have been treated. If this combination
does take place (mark what I say to you), you will
have meetings all over Ireland for the cry of *No*

Union ; that cry will spread like wild-fire, and blaze over every opposition; and if this be the case, there is no use in mincing the matter; Ireland is gone, and the death-blow of England is struck; and this event may happen *instantly*—before Mr. Canning and Mr. Hookham .Frere have turned Lord Howick's last speech into doggerel rhyme; before "*the near and dear relations*" have received another quarter of their pension, or Mr. Perceval conducted the Curates' Salary Bill safely to a third reading. If the mind of the English people, cursed as they now are with that madness of religious dissension which has been breathed into them for the purposes of private ambition, can be alarmed by any remembrances, and warned by any events, they should never forget how nearly Ireland was lost to this country during the American war; that it was saved merely by the jealousy of the Protestant Irish towards the Catholics, then a much more insignificant and powerless body than they now are. The Catholic and the Dissenter have since combined together against you. Last war, the winds, those ancient and unsubsidised allies of England; the winds, upon which English ministers depend as much for saving kingdoms as washerwomen do for drying clothes; the winds stood your friends: the French could only get into Ireland in small numbers, and the rebels were defeated. Since then, all the remaining kingdoms of Europe have been destroyed; and the Irish see that their national independence is gone, without having received any single one of those advantages which they were taught to

expect from the sacrifice. All good things were to
flow from the Union; they have none of them gained
anything. Every man's pride is wounded by it; no
man's interest is promoted. In the seventh year of
that union four million Catholics, lured by all kinds
of promises to yield up the separate dignity and sovereignty of their country, are forced to squabble with
such a man as Mr. Spencer Perceval for five thousand
pounds with which to educate their children in their
own mode of worship, he, the same Mr. Spencer,
having secured to his own Protestant self a reversionary portion of the public money amounting to four
times that sum. A senior Proctor of the University
of Oxford, the head of a house, or the examining
chaplain to a bishop, may believe these things can
last; but every man of the world, whose understanding
has been exercised in the business of life, must see
(and see with a breaking heart) that they will soon
come to a fearful termination.

Our conduct to Ireland during the whole of this
war has been that of a man who subscribes to hospitals,
weeps at charity sermons, carries out broth and blan-
kets to beggars, and then comes home and beats his
wife and children. We had compassion for the victims
of all other oppression and injustice except our own.
If Switzerland was threatened, away went a Treasury
Clerk with a hundred thousand pounds for Switzerland;
large bags of money were kept constantly under sailing
orders; upon the slightest demonstration towards
Naples, down went Sir William Hamilton upon his
knees, and begged for the love of St. Januarius they

would help us off with a little money; all the arts of
Machiavel were resorted to to persuade Europe to
borrow; troops were sent off in all directions to save
the Catholic and Protestant world; the Pope himself
was guarded by a regiment of English dragoons; if
the Grand Lama had been at hand, he would have had
another; every Catholic clergyman who had the good
fortune to be neither English nor Irish was immediately
provided with lodging, soap, crucifix, missal, chapel-
beads, relics, and holy water; if Turks had landed,
Turks would have received an order from the Treasury
for coffee, opium, korans, and seraglios. In the midst
of all this fury of saving and defending this crusade
for conscience and Christianity, there was a universal
agreement among all descriptions of people to continue
every species of internal persecution, to deny at home
every just right that had been denied before, to pum-
mel poor Dr. *Abraham Rees and his Dissenters, and
to treat the unhappy Catholics of Ireland as if their
tongues were mute, their heels cloven, their nature
brutal, and designedly subjected by Providence to
their Orange masters.

How would my admirable brother, the Rev. Abraham
Plymley, like to be marched to a Catholic chapel, to be
sprinkled with the sanctified contents of a pump, to
hear a number of false quantities in the Latin tongue,
and to see a number of persons occupied in making
right angles upon the breast and forehead? And if all
this would give you so much pain, what right have you
to march Catholic soldiers to a place of worship, where
there is no aspersion, no rectangular gestures, and

where they understand every word they hear, having
first, in order to get him to enlist, made a solemn promise to the contrary ?   Can you wonder, after this, that
the Catholic priest stops the recruiting in Ireland, as
he is now doing to a most alarming degree ?

The late question concerning military rank did not
individually affect the lowest persons of the Catholic
persuasion ; but do you imagine they do not sympa-
thise with the honour and disgrace of their superiors ?
Do you think that satisfaction and dissatisfaction do
not travel down from Lord Fingal to the most potato-
less Catholic in Ireland, and that the glory or shame of
the sect is not felt by many more than these conditions
personally and corporeally affect ?   Do you suppose that
the detection of Sir Henry Mildmay, and the disappointment of Mr. Perceval *in the matter* of the
Duchy of Lancaster, did not affect every dabbler in
public property ?   Depend upon it these things were
felt through all the gradations of small plunderers,
down to him who filches a pound of tobacco from the
King's warehouses ; while, on the contrary, the acquittal of any noble and official thief would not fail to
diffuse the most heart-felt satisfaction over the larcenous and burglarious world.   Observe, I do not say
because the lower Catholics are affected by what concerns their superiors, that they are not affected by
what concerns themselves.   There is no disguising the
horrid truth, *there must be some relaxation with respect to tithe :* this is the cruel and heart-rending price
which must be paid for national preservation.   I feel
how little existence will be worth having, if any altera-

tion, however slight, is made in the property of Irish rectors ; I am conscious how much such changes must affect the daily and hourly comforts of every Englishman ; I shall feel too happy if they leave Europe untouched, and are not ultimately fatal to the destinies of America ; but I am madly bent upon keeping foreign enemies out of the British empire, and my limited understanding presents me with no other means of effecting my object.

You talk of waiting till another reign before any alteration is made ; a proposal full of good sense and good nature, if the measure in question were to pull down St. James's Palace, or to alter Kew Gardens. Will Bonaparte agree to put off his intrigues, and his invasion of Ireland ? If so, I will overlook the question of justice, and finding the danger suspended, agree to the delay. I sincerely hope this reign may last many years, yet the delay of a single session of Parliament may be fatal ; but if another year elapse without some serious concession made to the Catholics, I believe, before God, that all future pledges and concessions will be made in vain. I do not think that peace will do you any good under such circumstances. If Bonaparte give you a respite, it will only be to get ready the gallows on which he means to hang you. The Catholic and the Dissenter can unite in peace as well as war. If they do, the gallows is ready, and your executioner, in spite of the most solemn promises, will turn you off the next hour.

With every disposition to please (where to please within fair and rational limits is a high duty), it is impossible for public men to be long silent about the Catholics; pressing evils are not got rid of, because they are not talked of. A man may command his family to say nothing more about the stone and surgical operations; but the ponderous malice still lies upon the nerve, and gets so big, that the patient breaks his own law of silence, clamours for the knife, and expires under its late operation. Believe me, you talk folly when you talk of suppressing the Catholic question. I wish to God the case admitted of such a remedy; bad as it is, it does not admit of it. If the wants of the Catholics are not heard in the manly tones of Lord Grenville, or the servile drawl of Lord Castlereagh, they will be heard ere long in the madness of mobs, and the conflicts of armed men.

I observe it is now universally the fashion to speak of the first personage in the state as the great obstacle to the measure. In the first place, I am not bound to believe such rumours because I hear them; and in the next place, I object to such language, as unconstitutional. Whoever retains his situation in the ministry while the incapacities of the Catholics remain, is the advocate for those incapacities; and to him, and to him only, am I to look for responsibility. But waive this question of the Catholics, and put a general case :—How is a minister of this country to act when the conscientious scruples of his Sovereign prevent the execution of a measure deemed by him absolutely necessary to the safety of the country? His conduct is quite clear—he should resign. But what is his successor to do?—Resign. But is the King to be

left without ministers, and is he in this manner to
be compelled to act against his own conscience? Before I answer this, pray tell me in my turn what better
defence is there against the machinations of a wicked,
or the errors of a weak Monarch, than the impossibility
of finding a minister who will lend himself to vice and
folly? Every English Monarch, in such a predicament, would sacrifice his opinions and views to such a
clear expression of the public will; and it is one method in which the Constitution aims at bringing about
such a sacrifice. You may say, if you please, the ruler
of a state is forced to give up his object when the
natural love of place and power will tempt no one to
assist him in its attainment; this may be force; but it
is force without injury, and therefore without blame.
I am not to be beat out of these obvious reasonings,
and ancient constitutional provisions, by the term conscience. There is no fantasy, however wild, that a man
may not persuade himself that he cherishes from
motives of conscience; eternal war against impious
France, or rebellious America, or Catholic Spain, may
in times to come be scruples of conscience. One
English Monarch may, from scruples of conscience,
wish to abolish every trait of religious persecution;
another Monarch may deem it his absolute and indispensable duty to make a slight provision for Dissenters
out of the revenues of the Church of England. So
that you see, Brother Abraham, there are cases where
it would be the duty of the best and most loyal subjects
to oppose the conscientious scruples of their Sovereign,
still taking care that their actions were constitutional

and their modes respectful. Then you come upon me
with personal questions, and say that no such dangers
are to be apprehended now under our present gracious
Sovereign, of whose good qualities we must be all so
well convinced. All these sorts of discussions I beg
leave to decline. What I have said upon constitutional
topics, I mean of course for general, not for particular
application. I agree with you in all the good you have
said of the powers that be, and I avail myself of the
opportunity of pointing out general dangers to the
Constitution, at a moment when we are so completely
exempted from their present influence. I cannot finish
this letter without expressing my surprise and pleasure
at your abuse of the servile addresses poured in upon
the throne, nor can I conceive a greater disgust to a
Monarch, with a true English heart, than to see such
a question as that of Catholic Emancipation argued,
not with a reference to its justice or importance, but
universally considered to be of no further consequence
than as it affects his own private feelings. That these
sentiments should be mine is not wonderful; but how
they came to be yours does, I confess, fill me with surprise. Are you moved by the arrival of the Irish
Brigade at Antwerp, and the amorous violence which
awaits Mrs. Plymley?

LETTER V.

DEAR ABRAHAM,—I never met a parson in my life
who did not consider the Corporation and Test Acts as
the great bulwarks of the Church; and yet it is now

just sixty-four years since bills of indemnity to destroy their penal effects, or, in other words, to repeal them, have been passed annually as a matter of course.

Heu ratum ignar mentes.

These bulwarks, without which no clergyman thinks he could sleep with his accustomed soundness, have actually not been in existence since any man now living has taken holy orders. Every year the Indemnity Act pardons past breaches of these two laws, and prevents any fresh actions of informers from coming to a conclusion before the period for the next indemnity bill arrives; so that these penalties, by which alone the Church remains in existence, have not had one moment's operation for sixty-four years. You will say the legislature, during the whole of this period, has reserved to itself the discretion of suspending or not suspending. But had not the legislature the right of re-enacting, if it was necessary? And now when you have kept the rod over these people (with the most scandalous abuse of all principle) for sixty-four years, and not found it necessary to strike once, is not that the best of all reasons why the rod should be laid aside? You talk to me of a very valuable hedge running across your fields which you would not part with on any account. I go down, expecting to find a limit impervious to cattle, and highly useful for the preservation of property; but, to my utter astonishment, I find that the hedge was cut down half a century ago, and that every year the shoots are clipped the moment they appear above ground: it appears, upon further inquiry, that the hedge never

ought to have existed at all; that it originated in the
malice of antiquated quarrels, and was cut down because it subjected you to vast inconvenience, and broke
up your intercourse with a country absolutely necessary
to your existence. If the remains of this hedge serve
only to keep up an irritation in your neighbours, and to
remind them of the feuds of former times, good nature
and good sense teach you that you ought to grub it up,
and cast it into the oven. This is the exact state of
these two laws; and yet it is made a great argument
against concession to the Catholics, that it involves
their repeal; which is to say, Do not make me relinquish
a folly that will lead to my ruin; because, if you do, I
must give up other follies ten times greater than this.

I confess, with all our bulwarks and hedges, it mor-
tifies me to the quick to contrast with our matchless
stupidity and inimitable folly the conduct of Bonaparte
upon the subject of religious persecution. At the
moment when we are tearing the crucifixes from the
necks of the Catholics, and washing pious mud from
the foreheads of the Hindoos; at that moment this man
is assembling the very Jews at Paris, and endeavouring to give them stability and importance. I shall
never be reconciled to mending shoes in America; but
I see it must be my lot, and I will then take a dreadful
revenge upon Mr. Perceval, if I catch him preaching
within ten miles of me. I cannot for the soul of me
conceive whence this man has gained his notions of
Christianity: he has the most evangelical charity for
errors in arithmetic, and the most inveterate malice
against errors in conscience. While he rages against

those whom in the true spirit of the Gospel he ought to
indulge, he forgets the only instance of severity which
that Gospel contains, and leaves the jobbers, contractors,
and money-changers at their seats, without a single
stripe.

You cannot imagine, you say, that England will ever
be ruined and conquered; and for no other reason that
I can find, but because it seems so very odd it should
be ruined and conquered. Alas! so reasoned, in their
time, the Austrian, Russian, and Prussian Plymleys.
But the English are brave: so were all these nations.
You might get together a hundred thousand men individually brave; but without generals capable of commanding such a machine, it would be as useless as a
first-rate man-of-war manned by Oxford clergymen or
Parisian shopkeepers. I do not say this to the dis-
paragement of English officers: they have had no
means of acquiring experience; but I do say it to create
alarm; for we do not appear to me to be half alarmed
enough, or to entertain that sense of our danger which
leads to the most obvious means of self-defence. As
for the spirit of the peasantry in making a gallant defence behind hedge-rows, and through plate-racks and
hen-coops, highly as I think of their bravery, I do not
know any nation in Europe so likely to be struck with
the panic as the English; and this from their total
unacquaintance with the science of war. Old wheat
and beans blazing for twenty miles round; cart mares
shot; sows of Lord Somerville's breed running wild
over the country; the minister of the parish wounded
sorely in his hinder parts; Mrs. Plymley in fits. All

these scenes of war an Austrian or a Russian has seen three or four times over : but it is now three centuries since an English pig has fallen in a fair battle upon English ground, or a farm-house been rifled, or a clergy-man's wife been subjected to any other proposals of love than the connubial endearments of her sleek and orthodox mate. The old edition of Plutarch's Lives, which lies in the corner of your parlour window, has contributed to work you up to the most romantic ex-pectations of our Roman behaviour. You are persuaded that Lord Amherst will defend Kew Bridge like Cocles; that some maid of honour will break away from her captivity, and swim over the Thames; that the Duke of York will burn his capitulating hand; and little Mr. Sturges Bourne give forty years' purchase for Moul-sham Hall, while the French are encamped upon it. I hope we shall witness all this, if the French do come ; but in the meantime I am so enchanted with the ordi-nary English behaviour of these invaluable persons, that I earnestly pray no opportunity may be given them for Roman valour, and for those very un-Roman pensions which they would all, of course, take especial care to claim in consequence. But whatever was our conduct, if every ploughman was as great a hero as he who was called from his oxen to save Rome from her enemies, I should still say, that at such a crisis you want the affections of all your subjects in both islands: there is no spirit which you must alienate, no art you must avert, every man must feel he has a country, and that there is an urgent and pressing cause why he should expose himself to death.

The effects of penal laws in matters of religion are never confined to those limits in which the legislature intended they should be placed: it is not only that I am excluded from certain offices and dignities because I am a Catholic, but the exclusion carries with it a certain stigma, which degrades me in the eyes of the monopolising sect, and the very name of my religion becomes odious. These effects are so very striking in England, that I solemnly believe blue and red baboons to be more popular here than Catholics and Presbyterians; they are more understood, and there is a greater disposition to do something for them. When a country squire hears of an ape, his first feeling is to give it nuts and apples; when he hears of a Dissenter, his immediate impulse is to commit it to the county gaol, to shave its head, to alter its customary food, and to have it privately whipped. This is no caricature, but an accurate picture of national feelings, as they degrade and endanger us at this very moment. The Irish Catholic gentleman would bear his legal disabilities with greater temper, if these were all he had to bear—if they did not enable every Protestant cheese-monger and tide-waiter to treat him with contempt. He is branded on the forehead with a red-hot iron, and treated like a spiritual felon, because in the highest of all considerations he is led by the noblest of all guides, his own disinterested conscience.

Why are nonsense and cruelty a bit the better because they are enacted? If Providence, which gives wine and oil, had blessed us with that tolerant spirit which makes the countenance more pleasant and the

heart more glad than these can do ; if our Statute Book
had never been defiled with such infamous laws, the
sepulchral Spencer Perceval would have been hauled
through the dirtiest horse-pond in Hampstead, had he
ventured to propose them.   But now persecution is
good, because it exists ; every law which originated in
ignorance and malice, and gratifies the passions from
whence it sprang, we call the wisdom of our ancestors :
when such laws are repealed, they will be cruelty and
madness ; till they are repealed, they are policy and
caution.

I was somewhat amused with the imputation brought
against the Catholics by the University of Oxford, that
they are enemies to liberty.   I immediately turned to my
"History of England," and marked as an historical
error that passage in which it is recorded that, in the
reign of Queen Anne, the famous degree of the University of Oxford respecting passive obedience, was
ordered by the House of Lords to be burnt by the
hands of the common hangman, as contrary to the liberty
of the subject and the law of the land.   Neverthe-
less, I wish, whatever be the modesty of those who
impute, that the imputation was a little more true, the
Catholic cause would not be quite so desperate with the
present Administration.   I fear, however, that the
hatred to liberty in these poor devoted wretches may
ere long appear more doubtful than it is at present to
the Vice-Chancellor and his Clergy, inflamed as they
doubtless are with classical examples of republican
virtue, and panting, as they always have been, to reduce
the power of the Crown within narrower and safer limits

What mistaken zeal to attempt to connect one religion with freedom and another with slavery! Who laid the foundations of English liberty? What was the mixed religion of Switzerland? What has the Protestant religion done for liberty in Denmark, in Sweden, throughout the north of Germany, and in Prussia? The purest religion in the world, in my humble opinion, is the religion of the Church of England: for its preservation (so far as it is exercised without intruding upon the liberties of others) I am ready at this moment to venture my present life, and but through that religion I have no hopes of any other; yet I am not forced to be silly because I am pious; nor will I ever join in eulogiums on my faith which every man of common reading and common sense can so easily refute.

You have either done too much for the Catholics, worthy Abraham, or too little; if you had intended to refuse them political power, you should have refused them civil rights. After you had enabled them to acquire property, after you had conceded to them all that you did concede in '78 and '93, the rest is wholly out of your power: you may choose whether you will give the rest in an honourable or a disgraceful mode, but it is utterly out of your power to withhold it.

In the last year, land to the amount of *eight hundred thousand pounds* was purchased by the Catholics in Ireland. Do you think it possible to be-Perceval, and be-Canning, and be-Castlereagh, such a body of men as this out of their common rights, and their common sense? Mr. George Canning may laugh and joke at the idea of Protestant bailiffs ravishing Catholic ladies, under the 9th clause of the Sunset Bill ; but if some better remedy be not applied to the distractions of Ireland than the jocularity of Mr. Canning, they will soon put an end to his pension, and to the pension of those "near and dear relatives," for whose eating, drinking, washing, and clothing, every man in the United Kingdoms now pays his twopence or three-pence a year. You may call these observations coarse, if you please ; but I have no idea that the Sophias and Carolines of any man breathing are to eat national veal, to drink public tea, to wear Treasury ribands, and then that we are to be told that it is coarse to ani-madvert upon this pitiful and eleemosynary splendour. If this is right, why not mention it ? If it is wrong, why should not he who enjoys the ease of supporting his sisters in this manner bear the shame of it ? Everybody seems hitherto to have spared a man who never spares anybody.

As for the enormous wax candles, and superstitious mummeries, and painted jackets of the Catholic priests, I fear them not. Tell me that the world will return again under the influence of the smallpox ; that Lord Castlereagh will hereafter oppose the power of the Court ; that Lord Howick and Mr. Grattan will do each of them a mean and dishonourable action ; that anybody who has heard Lord Redesdale speak once will knowingly and willingly hear him again ; that Lord Eldon has assented to the fact of two and two making four, without shedding tears, or expressing the smallest doubt or scruple ; tell me any other thing absurd or incredible, but, for the love of common

sense, let me hear no more of the danger to be apprehended from the general diffusion of Popery. It is
too absurd to be reasoned upon; every man feels it is
nonsense when he hears it stated, and so does every
man while he is stating it.

I cannot imagine why the friends to the Church
Establishment should entert in such a horror of seeing
the doors of Parliament flung open to the Catholics,
and view so passively the enjoyment of that right by
the Presbyterians and by every other species of Dissenter. In their tenets, in their Church Government,
in the nature of their endowments, the Dissenters are
infinitely more distant from the Church of England
than the Catholics are; yet the Dissenters have never
been excluded from Parliament. There are 45 members in one House, and 16 in the other, who always
are Dissenters. There is no law which would prevent
every member of the Lords and Commons from being
Dissenters. The Catholics could not bring into Parliament half the number of the Scotch members; and
yet one exclusion is of such immense importance,
because it has taken place; and the other no human
being thinks of, because no one is accustomed to it. I
have often thought, if the *wisdom of our ancestors* had
excluded all persons with red hair from the House of
Commons, of the throes and convulsions it would
occasion to restore them to their natural rights.
What mobs and riots would it produce! To what
infinite abuse and obloquy would the capillary patriot
be exposed; what wormwood would distil from Mr.
Perceval, what froth would drop from Mr. Canning;

how (I will not say *my*, but *our* Lord Hawkesbury,
for he belongs to us all)—how our Lord Hawkesbury
would work away about the hair of King William and
Lord Somers, and the authors of the great and
glorious Revolution; how Lord Eldon would appeal to
the Deity and his own virtues, and to the hair of his
children: some would say that red-haired men were
superstitious; some would prove they were atheists;
they would be petitioned against as the friends of
slavery, and the advocates for revolt; in short, such a
corruptor of the heart and understanding is the spirit
of persecution, that these unfortunate people (conspired
against by their fellow-subjects of every complexion),
if they did not emigrate to countries where hair of
another colour was persecuted, would be driven to
the falsehood of perukes, or the hypocrisy of the
Tricosian fluid.

As for the dangers of the Church (in spite of the
staggering events which have lately taken place), I
have not yet entirely lost my confidence in the power
of common sense, and I believe the Church to be in no
danger at all; but if it is, that danger is not from the
Catholics, but from the Methodists, and from that
patent Christianity which has been for some time
manufacturing at Clapham, to the prejudice of the old
and admirable article prepared by the Church. I
would counsel my lords the Bishops to keep their eyes
upon that holy village, and its vicinity; they will find
there a zeal in making converts far superior to anything which exists among the Catholics; a contempt
for the great mass of English clergy, much more

rooted and profound; and a regular fund to purchase livings for those groaning and garrulous gentlemen whom they denominate (by a standing sarcasm against the regular Church) Gospel preachers and vital clergy-men. I am too firm a believer in the general propriety and respectability of the English clergy, to believe they have much to fear either from old nonsense or from new; but if the Church must be supposed to be in danger, I prefer that nonsense which is grown half venerable from time, the force of which I have already tried and baffled, which at least has some excuse in the dark and ignorant ages in which it originated. The religious enthusiasm manufactured by living men before my own eyes disgusts my understanding as much, influences my imagination not at all, and excites my apprehensions much more.

I may have seemed to you to treat the situation of public affairs with some degree of levity; but I feel it deeply, and with nightly and daily anguish; because I know Ireland; I have known it all my life; I love it, and I foresee the crisis to which it will soon be exposed. Who can doubt but that Ireland will experience ulti-mately from France a treatment to which the conduct they have experienced from England is the love of a parent, or a brother? Who can doubt but that five years after he has got hold of the country, Ireland will be tossed away by Bonaparte as a present to some one of his ruffian generals, who will knock the head of Mr. Keogh against the head of Cardinal Troy, shoot twenty of the most noisy blockheads of the Roman persuasion, wash his pug-dogs in holy water, and

confiscate the salt butter of the Milesian republic to the
last tub?   But what matters this? or who is wise
enough in Ireland to heed it? or when had common
sense much influence with my poor dear Irish?   Mr.
Perceval does not know the Irish; but I know them,
and I know that at every rash and mad hazard they
will break the Union, revenge their wounded pride
and their insulted religion, and fling themselves into
the open arms of France, sure of dying in the em-
brace.   And now, what means have you of guarding
against this coming evil, upon which the future happiness or misery of every Englishman depends?   Have
you a single ally in the whole world?   Is there a
vulnerable point in the French empire where the
astonishing resources of that people can be attracted
and employed?   Have you a ministry wise enough to
comprehend the danger, manly enough to believe
unpleasant intelligence, honest enough to state their
apprehensions at the peril of their places?   Is there
anywhere the slightest disposition to join any measure of love, or conciliation, or hope, with that dreadful
bill which the distractions of Ireland have rendered
necessary?   At the very moment that the last Monarchy in Europe has fallen, are we not governed by a
man of pleasantry, and a man of theology?   In the
six hundredth year of our empire over Ireland, have
we any memorial of ancient kindness to refer to? any
people, any zeal, any country on which we can depend?
Have we any hope, but in the winds of heaven and
the tides of the sea? any prayer to prefer to the Irish,
but that they should forget and forgive their oppres-

sors, who, in the very moment that they are calling
upon them for their exertions, solemnly assure them
that the oppression shall still remain?

Abraham, farewell! If I have tired you, remember
how often you have tired me and others. I do not
think we really differ in politics so much as you
suppose; or at least, if we do, that difference is in the
means, and not in the end. We both love the Constitution, respect the King, and abhor the French. But
though you love the Constitution, you would perpe-
tuate the abuses which have been engrafted upon it;
though you respect the King, you would confirm his
scruples against the Catholics; though you abhor the
French, you would open to them the conquest of
Ireland. My method of respecting my sovereign is
by protecting his honour, his empire, and his lasting
happiness; I evince my love of the Constitution by
making it the guardian of all men's rights and the
source of their freedom; and I prove my abhorrence
of the French, by uniting against them the disciples
of every church in the only remaining nation in Europe.
As for the men of whom I have been compelled in this
age of mediocrity to say so much, they cannot of themselves be worth a moment's consideration, to you, to
me, or to anybody. In a year after their death they
will be forgotten as completely as if they had never
been; and are now of no further importance than as
they are the mere vehicles of carrying into effect the
common-place and mischievous prejudices of the times
in which they live.

C—46

LETTER VI.

DEAR ABRAHAM,—What amuses me the most is to hear
of the *indulgences* which the Catholics have received,
and their exorbitance in not being satisfied with those
indulgences : now if you complain to me that a man is
obtrusive and shameless in his requests, and that it
is impossible to bring him to reason, I must first of all
hear the whole of your conduct towards him; for you
may have taken from him so much in the first instance
that, in spite of a long series of restitution, a vast
latitude for petition may still remain behind.

There is a village, no matter where, in which the
inhabitants, on one day in the year, sit down to a
dinner prepared at the common expense : by an extraordinary piece of tyranny, which Lord Hawkesbury
would call the wisdom of the village ancestors, the inhabitants of three of the streets, about a hundred years
ago, seized upon the inhabitants of the fourth street,
bound them hand and foot, laid them upon their backs,
and compelled them to look on while the rest were
stuffing themselves with beef and beer; the next year
the inhabitants of the persecuted street, though they
contributed an equal quota of the expense, were treated
precisely in the same manner. The tyranny grew into a
custom; and, as the manner of our nature is, it was
considered as the most sacred of all duties to keep these
poor fellows without their annual dinner. The village was
so tenacious of this practice, that nothing could induce
them to resign it; every enemy to it was looked upon
as a disbeliever in Divine Providence, and any nefarious

churchwarden who wished to succeed in his election had nothing to do but to represent his antagonist as an abolitionist, in order to frustrate his ambition, endanger his life, and throw the village into a state of the most dreadful commotion. By degrees, however, the obnoxious street grew to be so well peopled, and its inhabitants so firmly united, that their oppressors, more afraid of injustice, were more disposed to be just. At the next dinner they are unbound, the year after allowed to sit upright, then a bit of bread and a glass of water; till at last, after a long series of concessions, they are emboldened to ask, in pretty plain terms, that they may be allowed to sit down at the bottom of the table, and to fill their bellies as well as the rest. Forthwith a general cry of shame and scandal: " Ten years ago, were you not laid upon your backs? Don't you remember what a great thing you thought it to get a piece of bread? How thankful you were for cheese parings? Have you forgotten that memorable era, when the lord of the manor interfered to obtain for you a slice of the public pudding? And now, with an audacity only equalled by your ingratitude, you have the impudence to ask for knives and forks, and to request, in terms too plain to be mistaken, that you may sit down to table with the rest, and be indulged even with beef and beer: there are not more than half a dozen dishes which we have reserved for ourselves; the rest has been thrown open to you in the utmost profusion; you have potatoes, and carrots, suet dumplings, sops in the pan, and delicious toast and water in incredible quantities. Beef, mutton, lamb, pork, and veal are ours; and if you were not the most restless and dissatisfied of human beings, you would never think of aspiring to enjoy them."

Is not this, my dainty Abraham, the very nonsense and the very insult which is talked to and practised upon the Catholics? You are surprised that men who have tasted of partial justice should ask for perfect justice; that he who has been robbed of coat and cloak will not be contented with the restitution of one of his garments. He would be a very lazy blockhead if he were content, and I (who, though an inhabitant of the village, have preserved, thank God, some sense of justice) most earnestly counsel these half-fed claimants to persevere in their just demands, till they are admitted to a more complete share of a dinner for which they pay as much as the others; and if they see a little attenuated lawyer squabbling at the head of their opponents, let them desire him to empty his pockets, and to pull out all the pieces of duck, fowl, and pudding which he has filched from the public feast, to carry home to his wife and children.

You parade a great deal upon the vast concessions made by this country to the Irish before the Union. I deny that any voluntary concession was ever made by England to Ireland. What did Ireland ever ask that was granted? What did she ever demand that was not refused? How did she get her Mutiny Bill—a limited Parliament—a repeal of Poyning's Law—a constitution? Not by the concessions of England, but by her fears. When Ireland asked for all these things upon her knees, her petitions were rejected with

Percevalism and contempt; when she demanded them
with the voice of 60,000 armed men, they were granted
with every mark of consternation and dismay. Ask of
Lord Auckland the fatal consequences of trifling with
such a people as the Irish. He himself was the organ
of these refusals. As secretary to the Lord Lieutenant,
the insolence and the tyranny of this country passed
through his hands. Ask him if he remembers the
consequences. Ask him if he has forgotten that
memorable evening when he came down booted and
mantled to the House of Commons, when he told the
House he was about to set off for Ireland that
night, and declared before God, if he did not carry
with him a compliance with all their demands, Ireland
was for ever lost to this country. The present generation have forgotten this; but I have not forgotten it;
and I know, hasty and undignified as the submission
of England then was, that Lord Auckland was right,
that the delay of a single day might very probably
have separated the two peoples for ever. The terms
submission and fear are galling terms when applied
from the lesser nation to the greater; but it is the plain
historical truth, it is the natural consequence of injustice, it is the predicament in which every country
places itself which leaves such a mass of hatred and
discontent by its side. No empire is powerful enough
to endure it; it would exhaust the strength of China,
and sink it with all its mandarins and tea-kettles to the
bottom of the deep. By refusing them justice now
when you are strong enough to refuse them anything
more than justice, you will act over again, with the

Catholics, the same scene of mean and precipitate submission which disgraced you before America, and before the volunteers of Ireland. We shall live to hear the Hampstead Protestant pronouncing such extravagant panegyrics upon holy water, and paying such fulsome compliments to the thumbs and offals of departed saints, that parties will change sentiments, and Lord Henry Petty and Sam Whitbread take a spell at No Popery. The wisdom of Mr. Fox was alike employed in teaching his country justice when Ireland was weak, and dignity when Ireland was strong. We are fast pacing round the same miserable circle of ruin and imbecility. Alas! where is our guide?

You say that Ireland is a millstone about our necks; that it would be better for us if Ireland were sunk at the bottom of the sea; that the Irish are a nation of irreclaimable savages and barbarians. How often have I heard these sentiments fall from the plump and thoughtless squire, and from the thriving English shopkeeper, who has never felt the rod of an Orange master upon his back. Ireland a millstone about your neck! Why is it not a stone of Ajax in your hand? I agree with you most cordially that, governed as Ireland now is, it would be a vast accession of strength if the waves of the sea were to rise and engulf her to-morrow. At this moment, opposed as we are to all the world, the annihilation of one of the most fertile islands on the face of the globe, containing five millions of human creatures, would be one of the most solid advantages which could happen to this country. I doubt very much, in spite of all the just abuse which has been lavished upon Bonaparte, whether there is any one of his conquered countries the blotting out of which would be as beneficial to him as the destruction of Ireland would be to us: of countries I speak differing in language from the French, little habituated to their intercourse, and inflamed with all the resentments of a recently-conquered people. Why will you attribute the turbulence of our people to any cause but the right—to any cause but your own scandalous oppression? If you tie your horse up to a gate, and beat him cruelly, is he vicious because he kicks you? If you have plagued and worried a mastiff dog for years, is he mad because he flies at you whenever he sees you? Hatred is an active, troublesome passion. Depend upon it, whole nations have always some reason for their hatred. Before you refer the turbulence of the Irish to incurable defects in their character, tell me if you have treated them as friends and equals? Have you protected their commerce? Have you respected their religion? Have you been as anxious for their freedom as your own? Nothing of all this. What then? Why you have confiscated the territorial surface of the country twice over: you have massacred and exported her inhabitants: you have deprived four-fifths of them of every civil privilege: you have at every period made her commerce and manufactures slavishly subordinate to your own: and yet the hatred which the Irish bear to you is the result of an original turbulence of character, and of a primitive, obdurate wildness, utterly incapable of civilisation. The embroidered inanities and the sixth-form effusions of Mr. Canning

are really not powerful enough to make me believe
this; nor is there any authority on earth (always
excepting the Dean of Christ Church) which could
make it credible to me. I am sick of Mr. Canning.
There is not a "ha'porth of bread to all this sugar
and sack." I love not the cretaceous and incredible
countenance of his colleague. The only opinion in
which I agree with these two gentlemen is that which
they entertain of each other. I am sure that the insolence of Mr. Pitt, and the unbalanced accounts of
Melville, were far better than the perils of this new
ignorance :—

> Nonne fuit satiùs, ristes Amaryllidis iras
> Atque superba pati fastidia? nonne Menalcan?
> Quamvis ille *niger?*

In the midst of the most profound peace, the secret
articles of the Treaty of Tilsit, in which the destruction of Ireland is resolved upon, induce you to rob the
Danes of their fleet. After the expedition sailed comes
the Treaty of Tilsit, containing no article, public or
private, alluding to Ireland. The state of the world,
you tell me, justified us in doing this. Just God! do
we think only of the state of the world when there
is an opportunity for robbery, for murder, and for
plunder; and do we forget the state of the world when
we are called upon to be wise, and good, and just?
Does the state of the world never remind us that we
have four millions of subjects whose injuries we ought
to atone for, and whose affections we ought to conciliate? Does the state of the world never warn us to
lay aside our infernal bigotry, and to arm every man

who acknowledges a God, and can grasp a sword?
Did it never occur to this administration that they
might virtuously get hold of a force ten times greater
than the force of the Danish fleet? Was there no
other way of protecting Ireland but by bringing
eternal shame upon Great Britain, and by making the
earth a den of robbers? See what the men whom you
have supplanted would have done. They would have
rendered the invasion of Ireland impossible, by restor-
ing to the Catholics their long-lost rights: they would
have acted in such a manner that the French would
neither have wished for invasion nor dared to attempt
it: they would have increased the permanent strength
of the country while they preserved its reputation un-
sullied. Nothing of this kind your friends have done,
because they are solemnly pledged to do nothing of this
kind; because, to tolerate all religions, and to equalise
civil rights to all sects, is to oppose some of the worst
passions of our nature—to plunder and to oppress is to
gratify them all. They wanted the huzzas of mobs,
and they have for ever blasted the fame of England to.
obtain them. Were the fleets of Holland, France, and
Spain destroyed by larceny? You resisted the power
of 150 sail of the line by sheer courage, and violated
every principle of morals from the dread of fifteen hulks,
while the expedition itself cost you three times more
than the value of the larcenous matter brought away.
The French trample on the laws of God and man, not
for old cordage, but for kingdoms, and always take care
to be well paid for their crimes. We contrive, under
the present administration, to unite moral with intel-

lectual deficiency, and to grow weaker and worse by the
same action.   If they had any evidence of the intended
hostility of the Danes, why was it not produced? Why
have the nations of Europe been allowed to feel an indignation against this country beyond the reach of all
subsequent information?   Are these times, do you
imagine, when we can trifle with a year of universal
hatred, dally with the curses of Europe, and then re-
gain a lost character at pleasure, by the parliamentary
perspirations of the Foreign Secretary, or the solemn
asseverations of the pecuniary Rose? Believe me,
Abraham, it is not under such ministers as these that
the dexterity of honest Englishmen will ever equal
the dexterity of French knaves; it is not in their
presence that the serpent of Moses will ever swallow
up the serpents of the magician.

Lord Hawkesbury says that nothing is to be granted
to the Catholics from fear.   What! not even justice?
Why not? There are four millions of disaffected people
within twenty miles of your own coast. I fairly confess
that the dread which I have of their physical power is
with me a very strong motive for listening to their
claims.   To talk of not acting from fear, is mere parliamentary cant.   From what motive but fear, I should
be glad to know, have all the improvements in our constitution proceeded?   I question if any justice has ever
been done to large masses of mankind from any other
motive.   By what other motives can the plunderers of
the Baltic suppose nations to be governed in their intercourse *with each other?* If I say, Give this people
what they ask because it is just, do you think I should

get ten people to listen to me? Would not the lesser of the two Jenkinsons be the first to treat me with contempt? The only true way to make the mass of mankind see the beauty of justice is by showing to them, in pretty plain terms, the consequences of injustice. If any body of French troops land in Ireland, the whole population of that country will rise against you to a man, and you could not possibly survive such an event three years. Such, from the bottom of my soul, do I believe to be the present state of that country; and so far does it appear to me to be impolitic and unstatesman-like to concede anything to such a danger, that if the Catholics, in addition to their present just demands, were to petition for the perpetual removal of the said Lord Hawkesbury from his Majesty's councils, I think, whatever might be the effect upon the destinies of Europe, and however it might retard our own individual destruction, that the prayer of the petition should be instantly complied with. Canning's crocodile tears should not move me; the hoops of the maids of honour should not hide him. I would tear him from the banisters of the back stairs, and plunge him in the fishy fumes of the dirtiest of all his Cinque Ports.

LETTER VII.

DEAR ABRAHAM,—In the correspondence which is passing between us, you are perpetually alluding to the Foreign Secretary; and in answer to the dangers of Ireland, which I am pressing upon your notice, you have nothing to urge but the confidence which you

repose in the discretion and sound sense of this gentleman. I can only say, that I have listened to him long
and often with the greatest attention; I have used
every exertion in my power to take a fair measure of
him, and it appears to me impossible to hear him upon
any arduous topic without perceiving that he is eminently deficient in those solid and serious qualities
upon which, and upon which alone, the confidence of a
great country can properly repose. He sweats and
labours, and works for sense, and Mr. Ellis seems
always to think it is coming, but it does not come; the
machine can't draw up what is not to be found in the
spring; Providence has made him a light, jesting,
paragraph-writing man, and that he will remain to his
dying day. When he is jocular he is strong, when he
is serious he is like Samson in a wig; any ordinary
person is a match for him : a song, an ironical letter,
a burlesque ode, an attack in the newspaper upon
Nicoll's eye, a smart speech of twenty minutes, full of
gross misrepresentations and clever turns, excellent
language, a spirited manner, lucky quotation, success
in provoking dull men, some half information picked
up in Pall Mall in the morning; these are your
friend's natural weapons; all these things he can do :
here I allow him to be truly great ; nay, I will be just,
and go still further, if he would confine himself to these
things, and consider the *facete* and the playful to be
the basis of his character, he would, for that species of
man, be universally regarded as a person of a very good
understanding ; call him a legislator, a reasoner, and the
conductor of the affairs of a great nation, and it seems

to me as absurd as if a butterfly were to teach bees to make honey. That he is an extraordinary writer of small poetry, and a diner out of the highest lustre, I do most readily admit. After George Selwyn, and perhaps Tickell, there has been no such man for this half-century. The Foreign Secretary is a gentleman, a respectable as well as a highly agreeable man in private life; but you may as well feed me with decayed potatoes as console me for the miseries of Ireland by the resources of his *sense* and his *discretion.* It is only the public situation which this gentleman holds which entitles me or induces me to say so much about him. He is a fly in amber, nobody cares about the fly; the only question is, How the devil did it get there? Nor do I attack him for the love of glory, but from the love of utility, as a burgomaster hunts a rat in a Dutch dyke, for fear it should flood a province.

The friends of the Catholic question are, I observe, extremely embarrassed in arguing when they come to the loyalty of the Irish Catholics. As for me, I shall go straight forward to my object, and state what I have no manner of doubt, from an intimate knowledge of Ireland, to be the plain truth. Of the great Roman Catholic proprietors, and of the Catholic prelates, there may be a few, and but a few, who would follow the fortunes of England at all events : there is another set of men who, thoroughly detesting this country, have too much property and too much character to lose, not to wait for some very favourable event before they show themselves; but the great mass of Catholic population, upon the slightest appearance of a French

force in that country, would rise upon you to a man.
It is the most mistaken policy to conceal the plain
truth. There is no loyalty among the Catholics : they
detest you as their worst oppressors, and they will continue to detest you till you remove the cause of their
hatred. It is in your power in six months' time to
produce a total revolution of opinions among this
people; and in some future letter I will show you that
this is clearly the case. At present, see what a dreadful
state Ireland is in. The common toast among the low
Irish is, the feast of the *passover*. Some allusion to
Bonaparte, in a play lately acted at Dublin, produced
thunders of applause from the pit and the galleries ;
and a politician should not be inattentive to the public
feelings expressed in theatres. Mr. Perceval thinks he
has disarmed the Irish : he has no more disarmed the
Irish than he has resigned a shilling of his own public
emoluments. An Irish peasant fills the barrel of his
gun full of tow dipped in oil, butters up the lock,
buries it in a bog, and allows the Orange bloodhound
to ransack his cottage at pleasure. Be just and kind
to the Irish, and you will indeed disarm them ; rescue
them from the degraded servitude in which they are
held by a handful of their own countrymen, and you
will add four millions of brave and affectionate men to
your strength. Nightly visits, Protestant inspectors,
licenses to possess a pistol, or a knife and fork, the
odious vigour of the *evangelical* Perceval—acts of
Parliament, drawn up by some English attorney, to
save you from the hatred of four millions of people—
the guarding yourselves from universal disaffection by

a police; a confidence in the little cunning of Bow Street, when you might rest your security upon the eternal basis of the best feelings : this is the meanness and madness to which nations are reduced when they lose sight of the first elements of justice, without which a country can be no more secure than it can be healthy without air. I sicken at such policy and such men. The fact is, the Ministers know nothing about the present state of Ireland; Mr. Perceval sees a few clergymen, Lord Castlereagh a few general officers, who take care, of course, to report what is pleasant rather than what is true. As for the joyous and lepid consul, he jokes upon neutral flags and frauds, jokes upon Irish rebels, jokes upon northern and western and southern foes, and gives himself no trouble upon any subject; nor is the mediocrity of the idolatrous deputy of the slightest use. Dissolved in grins, he reads no memorials upon the state of Ireland, listens to no reports, asks no questions, and is the

"*Bourn* from whom no traveller returns."

The danger of an immediate insurrection is now, I *believe*, blown over. You have so strong an army in Ireland, and the Irish are become so much more cunning from the last insurrection, that you may perhaps be tolerably secure just at present from that evil : but are you secure from the efforts which the French may make to throw a body of troops into Ireland ? and do you consider that event to be difficult and improbable ? From Brest Harbour to Cape St. Vincent, you have above three thousand miles of hostile sea coast, and twelve or fourteen harbours quite capable of containing a sufficient force for the powerful invasion of Ireland. The nearest of these harbours is not two days' sail from the southern coast of Ireland, with a fair leading wind; and the furthest not ten. Five ships of the line, for so very short a passage, might carry five or six thousand troops with cannon and ammunition; and Ireland presents to their attack a southern coast of more than 500 miles, abounding in deep bays, admirable harbours, and disaffected inhabitants. Your blockading ships may be forced to come home for provisions and repairs, or they may be blown off in a gale of wind and compelled to bear away for their own coast; and you will observe that the very same wind which locks you up in the British Channel, when you are got there, is evidently favourable for the invasion of Ireland. And yet this is called Government, and the people huzza Mr. Perceval for continuing to expose his country day after day to such tremendous perils as these; cursing the men who would have given up a question in theology to have saved us from such a risk. The British empire at this moment is in the state of a peach-blossom—if the wind blows gently from one quarter, it survives; if furiously from the other, it perishes. A stiff breeze may set in from the north, the Rochefort squadron will be taken, and the Minister will be the most holy of men: if it comes from some other point, Ireland is gone; we curse ourselves as a set of monastic madmen, and call out for the unavailing satisfaction of Mr. Perceval's head. Such a state of political existence is scarcely credible: it is the action of a mad young fool standing upon one foot, and peeping down the crater of Mount Ætna, not the conduct of a wise and sober people deciding upon their best and dearest interests : and in the name, the much-injured name, of heaven, what is it all for that we expose ourselves to these dangers? Is it that we may sell more muslin? Is it that we may acquire more territory? Is it that we may strengthen what we have already acquired? No; nothing of all this; but that one set of Irishmen may torture another set of Irishmen—that Sir Phelim O'Callaghan may continue to whip Sir Toby M'Tackle, his next door neighbour, and continue to ravish his Catholic daughters; and these are the measures which the honest and consistent Secretary supports; and this is the Secretary whose genius in the estimation of Brother Abraham is to extinguish the genius of Bonaparte. Pompey was killed by a slave, Goliath smitten by a stripling, Pyrrhus died by the hand of a woman; tremble, thou great Gaul, from whose head an armed Minerva leaps forth in the hour of danger; tremble, thou scourge of God, a pleasant man is come out against thee, and thou shalt be laid low by a joker of jokes, and he shall talk his pleasant talk against thee, and thou shalt be no more!

You tell me, in spite of all this parade of sea-coast, Bonaparte has neither ships nor sailors: but this is a mistake. He has not ships and sailors to contest the empire of the seas with Great Britain, but there remains quite sufficient of the navies of France, Spain, Holland, and Denmark, for these short excursions and invasions. Do you think, too, that Bonaparte does not

add to his navy every year? Do you suppose, with
all Europe at his feet, that he can find any difficulty
in obtaining timber, and that money will not procure
for him any quantity of naval stores he may want?
The mere machine, the empty ship, he can build as
well, and as quickly, as you can; and though he may
not find enough of practised sailors to man large
fighting-fleets—it is not possible to conceive that he
can want sailors for such sort of purposes as I have
stated. He is at present the despotic monarch of
above twenty thousand miles of sea-coast, and yet you
suppose he cannot procure sailors for the invasion of
Ireland. Believe, if you please, that such a fleet met
at sea by any number of our ships at all comparable
to them in point of force, would be immediately taken,
let it be so; I count nothing upon their power of resistance, only upon their power of escaping unobserved.
If experience has taught us anything, it is the impossibility of perpetual blockades. The instances are
innumerable, during the course of this war, where
whole fleets have sailed in and out of harbour, in spite
of every vigilance used to prevent it. I shall only
mention those cases where Ireland is concerned. In
December, 1796, seven ships of the line, and ten trans-
ports, reached Bantry Bay from Brest, without having
seen an English ship in their passage. It blew a
storm when they were off shore, and therefore England still continues to be an independent kingdom.
You will observe that at the very time the French
fleet sailed out of Brest Harbour, Admiral Colpoys
was cruising off there with a powerful squadron, and

s.ill, from the particular circumstances of the weather, found it impossible to prevent the French from coming out. During the time that Admiral Colpoys was cruising off Brest, Admiral Richery, with six ships of the line, passed him, and got safe into the harbour. At the very moment when the French squadron was lying in Bantry Bay, Lord Bridport with his fleet was locked up by a foul wind in the Channel, and for several days could not stir to the assistance of Ireland. Admiral Colpoys, totally unable to find the French fleet, came home. Lord Bridport, at the change of the wind, cruised for them in vain, and they got safe back to Brest, without having seen a single one of those floating bulwarks, the possession of which we believe will enable us with impunity to set justice and common sense at defiance. Such is the miserable and precarious state of an anemocracy, of a people who put their trust in hurricanes, and are governed by wind. In August, 1798, three forty-gun frigates landed 1,100 men under Humbert, making the passage from Rochelle to Killala without seeing any English ship. In October of the same year, four French frigates anchored in Killala Bay with 2,000 troops; and though they did not land their troops, they returned to France in safety. In the same month, a line-of-battle ship, eight stout frigates, and a brig, all full of troops and stores, reached the coast of Ireland, and were fortunately, in sight of land, destroyed, after an obstinate engagement, by Sir John Warren.

If you despise the little troop which, in these

numerous experiments, did make good its landing, take with you, if you please, this *précis* of its exploits: eleven hundred men, commanded by a soldier raised from the ranks, put to rout a select army of 6,000 men, commanded by General Lake, seized their ordnance, ammunition, and stores, advanced 150 miles into a country containing an armed force of 150,000 men, and at last surrendered to the Viceroy, an experienced general, gravely and cautiously advancing at the head of all his chivalry and of an immense army to oppose him. You must excuse these details about Ireland, but it appears to me to be of all other subjects the most important. If we conciliate Ireland, we can do nothing amiss; if we do not, we can do nothing well. If Ireland was friendly, we might equally set at defiance the talents of Bonaparte and the blunders of his rival, Mr. Canning; we could then support the ruinous and silly bustle of our useless expeditions, and the almost incredible ignorance of our commercial orders in council. Let the present administration give up but this one point, and there is nothing which I would not consent to grant them. Mr. Perceval shall have full liberty to insult the tomb of Mr. Fox, and to torment every eminent Dissenter in Great Britain; Lord Camden shall have large boxes of plums; Mr. Rose receive permission to prefix to his name the appellative of virtuous; and to the Viscount Castlereagh a round sum of ready money shall be well and truly paid into his hand. Lastly, what remains to Mr. George Canning, but that he ride up and down Pall Mall glorious upon a white horse, and that they

cry out before him, Thus shall it be done to the states-
man who hath written "The Needy Knife-Grinder,"
and the German play? Adieu only for the present;
you shall soon hear from me again; it is a subject
upon which I cannot long be silent.

LETTER VIII.

NOTHING can be more erroneous than to suppose that
Ireland is not bigger than the Isle of Wight, or of
more consequence than Guernsey or Jersey; and yet
I am almost inclined to believe, from the general
supineness which prevails here respecting the dangerous
state of that country, that such is the rank which it
holds in our statistical tables. I have been writing to
you a great deal about Ireland, and perhaps it may be
of some use to state to you concisely the nature and
resources of the country which has been the subject of
our long and strange correspondence. There were
returned, as I have before observed, to the hearth tax
in 1791, 701,102 houses, which Mr. Newenham shows
from unquestionable documents to be nearly 80,000
below the real number of houses in that country.
There are 27,457 square English miles in Ireland, and
more than five millions of people. .

By the last survey it appears that the inhabited
houses in England and Wales amount to 1,574,902,
and the population to 9,343,578, which gives an
average of $5\frac{7}{8}$ to each house, in a country where the
density of population is certainly less considerable
than in Ireland. It is commonly supposed that two-

fifths of the army and navy are Irishmen, at periods
when political disaffection does not avert the Catholics
from the service. The current value of Irish exports
in 1807 was £9,314,854 17s. 7d.; a state of commerce
about equal to the commerce of England in the middle
of the reign of George II. The tonnage of ships
entered inward and cleared outward in the trade of
Ireland, in 1807, amounted to 1,567,430 tons. The
quantity of home spirits exported amounted to 10,284
gallons in 1796, and to 930,800 gallons in 1804. Of
the exports which I have stated, provisions amounted
to four millions, and linen to about four millions and
a half. There was exported from Ireland, upon an
average of two years ending in January, 1804, 591,274
barrels of barley, oats, and wheat; and by weight
910,848 cwts. of flour, oatmeal, barley, oats, and wheat.
The amount of butter exported in 1804, from Ireland,
was worth, in money, £1,704,680 sterling. The importation of ale and beer, from the immense manufactures now carrying on of these articles, was
diminished to 3,209 barrels, in the year 1804, from
111,920 barrels, which was the average importation per
annum, taking from three years ending in 1792; and
at present there is an export trade of porter. On an
average of three years, ending March, 1783, there were
imported into Ireland, of cotton wool, 3,326 cwts., of
cotton yarn, 5,405 lbs.; but on an average of three
years, ending January, 1803, there were imported, of
the first article, 13,159 cwts., and of the latter,
628,406 lbs. It is impossible to conceive any manufacture more flourishing. The export of linen has

increased in Ireland from 17,776,862 yards, the
average in 1770, to 43,534,971 yards, the amount in
1805. The tillage of Ireland has more than trebled
within the last twenty-one years. The importation of
coals has increased from 230,000 tons in 1783, to
417,030 in 1804; of tobacco, from 3,459,861 lbs. in
1783, to 6,611,543 in 1804; of tea, from 1,703,855 lbs.
in 1783, to 3,358,256 in 1804; of sugar, from 143,117
cwts. in 1782, to 309,076 in 1804. Ireland now
supports a funded debt of above 64 millions, and it is
computed that more than three millions of money are
annually remitted to Irish absentees resident in this
country. In Mr. Foster's report, of 100 folio pages,
presented to the House of Commons in the year 1806,
the total expenditure of Ireland is stated at £9,760,013.
Ireland has increased about two-thirds in its population within twenty-five years, and yet, and in about
the same space of time, its exports of beef, bullocks,
cows, pork, swine, butter, wheat, barley, and oats,
collectively taken, have doubled; and this, in spite of
two years' famine, and the presence of an immense
army, that is always at hand to guard the most
valuable appanage of our empire from joining our most
inveterate enemies. Ireland has the greatest possible
facilities for carrying on commerce with the whole of
Europe. It contains, within a circuit of 750 miles,
66 secure harbours, and presents a western frontier
against Great Britain, reaching from the Firth of
Clyde north to the Bristol Channel south, and varying
in distance from 20 to 100 miles; so that the subjugation of Ireland would compel us to guard with ships

and soldiers a new line of coast, certainly amounting, with all its sinuosities, to more than 700 miles—an addition of polemics, in our present state of hostility with all the world, which must highly gratify the vigorists, and give them an ample opportunity of displaying that foolish energy upon which their claims to distinction are founded. Such is the country which the Right Reverend the Chancellor of the Exchequer would drive into the arms of France, and for the conciliation of which we are requested to wait, as if it were one of those sinecure places which were given to Mr. Perceval snarling at the breast, and which cannot be abolished till his decease.

How sincerely and fervently have I often wished that the Emperor of the French had thought as Mr. Spencer Perceval does upon the subject of government; that he had entertained doubts and scruples upon the propriety of admitting the Protestants to an equality of rights with the Catholics, and that he had left in the middle of his empire these vigorous seeds of hatred and disaffection! But the world was never yet conquered by a blockhead. One of the very first measures we saw him recurring to was the complete establishment of religious liberty : if his subjects fought and paid as he pleased, he allowed them to believe as they pleased : the moment I saw this, my best hopes were lost. I perceived in a moment the kind of man we had to do with. I was well aware of the miserable ignorance and folly of this country upon the subject of toleration; and every year has been adding to the success of that game, which it was

clear he had the will and the ability to play against
us.

You say Bonaparte is not in earnest upon the subject
of religion, and that this is the cause of his tolerant
spirit; but is it possible you can intend to give us
such dreadful and unamiable notions of religion. Are
we to understand that the moment a man is sincere he
is narrow-minded; that persecution is the child of
belief; and that a desire to leave all men in the quiet
and unpunished exercise of their own creed can only
exist in the mind of an infidel? Thank God! I know
many men whose principles are as firm as they are
expanded, who cling tenaciously to their own modification of the Christian faith, without the slightest disposition to force that modification upon other people.
If Bonaparte is liberal in subjects of religion because
he has no religion, is this a reason why we should be
illiberal because we are Christians? If he owes this
excellent quality to a vice, is that any reason why we
may not owe it to a virtue? Toleration is a great
good, and a good to be imitated, let it come from
whom it will. If a sceptic is tolerant, it only shows
that he is not foolish in practice as well as erroneous in
theory. If a religious man is tolerant, it evinces that
he is religious from thought and inquiry, because he
exhibits in his conduct one of the most beautiful and
important consequences of a religious mind—an in-
violable charity to all the honest varieties of human
opinion.

Lord Sidmouth, and all the anti-Catholic people,
little foresee that they will hereafter be the sport of

the antiquary; that their prophecies of ruin and destruction from Catholic emancipation will be clapped into the notes of some quaint history, and be matter of pleasantry even to the sedulous housewife and the rural dean. There is always a copious supply of Lord Sidmouths in the world ; nor is there one single source of human happiness against which they have not uttered the most lugubrious predictions. Turnpike roads, navigable canals, inoculation, hops, tobacco, the Reformation, the Revolution—there are always a set of worthy and moderately-gifted men, who bawl out death and ruin upon every valuable change which the varying aspect of human affairs absolutely and imperiously requires. I have often thought that it would be extremely useful to make a collection of the hatred and abuse that all those changes have experienced, which are now admitted to be marked improvements in our condition. Such a history might make folly a little more modest, and suspicious of its own decisions.

Ireland, you say, since the Union is to be considered as a part of the whole kingdom ; and therefore, however Catholics may predominate in that particular spot, yet, taking the whole empire together, they are to be considered as a much more insignificant quota of the population. Consider them in what light you please, as part of the whole, or by themselves, or in what manner may be most consentaneous to the devices of your holy mind—I say in a very few words, if you do not relieve these people from the civil incapacities to which they are exposed, you will lose them ; or you must employ great strength and much treasure in watching over them. In the present state of the world you can afford to do neither the one nor the other. Having stated this, I shall leave you to be ruined, Puffendorf in hand (as. Mr. Secretary Canning says), and to lose Ireland, just as you have found out what proportion the aggrieved people should bear to the whole population before their calamities meet with redress. As for your parallel cases, I am no more afraid of deciding upon them than I am upon their prototype. If ever any one heresy should so far spread itself over the principality of Wales that the Established Church were left in a minority of one to four; if you had subjected these heretics to very severe civil privations; if the consequence of such privations were a universal state of disaffection among that caseous and wrathful people; and if at the same time you were at war with all the world, how can you doubt for a moment that I would instantly restore them to a state of the most complete civil liberty? What matters it under what name you put the same case? Common sense is not changed by appellations. I have said how I would act to Ireland, and I would act so to all the world.

I admit that, to a certain degree, the Government will lose the affections of the Orangemen by emancipating the Catholics; much less, however, at present, than three years past. The few men, who have ill-treated the whole crew, live in constant terror that the oppressed people will rise upon them and carry the ship into Brest:—they begin to find that it is a very tiresome thing to sleep every night with cocked pistols under

their pillows, and to breakfast, dine, and sup with
drawn hangers. They suspect that the privilege of
beating and kicking the rest of the sailors is hardly
worth all this anxiety, and that if the ship does ever
fall into the hands of the disaffected, all the cruelties
which they have experienced will be thoroughly remembered and amply repaid. To a short period of
disaffection among the Orangemen I confess I should
not much object : my love of poetical justice does carry
me as far as that ; one summer's whipping, only one :
the thumb-screw for a short season ; a little light easy
torturing between Ladyday and Michaelmas ; a short
specimen of Mr. Perceval's rigour. I have malice
enough to ask this slight atonement for the groans and
shrieks of the poor Catholics, unheard by any human
tribunal, but registered by the Angel of God against
their Protestant and enlightened oppressors.

Besides, if you who count ten so often can count five,
you must perceive that it is better to have four friends
and one enemy than four enemies and one friend ; and
the more violent the hatred of the Orangemen, the
more certain the reconciliation of the Catholics. The
disaffection of the Orangemen will be the Irish rain-
bow : when I see it I shall be sure that the storm is
over.

If these incapacities, from which the Catholics ask
to be relieved, were to the mass of them only a mere
feeling of pride, and if the question were respecting
the attainment of privileges which could be of importance only to the highest of the sect, I should still say
that the pride of the mass was very naturally wounded

by the degradation of their superiors. Indignity to
George Rose would be felt by the smallest nummary
gentleman in the king's employ; and Mr. John Ban-
nister could not be indifferent to anything which happened to Mr. Canning. But the truth is, it is a most
egregious mistake to suppose that the Catholics are
contending merely for the fringes and feathers of their
chiefs. I will give you a list in my next Letter of those
privations which are represented to be of no consequence
to anybody but Lord Fingal, and some twenty or thirty
of the principal persons of their sect. In the meantime, adieu, and be wise.

LETTER IX.

DEAR ABRAHAM,—No Catholic can be chief Governor
or Governor of this kingdom, Chancellor or Keeper of
the Great Seal, Lord High Treasurer, Chief of any of
the Courts of Justice, Chancellor of the Exchequer,
Puisne Judge, Judge in the Admiralty, Master of the
Rolls, Secretary of State, Keeper of the Privy Seal,
Vice-Treasurer or his Deputy, Teller or Cashier of
Exchequer, Auditor or General, Governor or Custos
Rotulorum of Counties, Chief Governor's Secretary,
Privy Councillor, King's Counsel, Serjeant, Attorney,
Solicitor-General, Master in Chancery, Provost or Fel-
low of Trinity College, Dublin, Postmaster-General,
Master and Lieutenant-General of Ordnance, Com-
mander-in-Chief, General on the Staff, Sheriff, Sub-
Sheriff, Mayor, Bailiff, Recorder, Burgess, or any other
officer in a City, or a Corporation. No Catholic can be

guardian to a Protestant, and no priest guardian at all;
no Catholic can be a gamekeeper, or have for sale, or
otherwise, any arms or warlike stores; no Catholic can
present to a living, unless he choose to turn Jew in
order to obtain that privilege; the pecuniary qualifi-
cation of Catholic jurors is made higher than that of
Protestants, and no relaxation of the ancient rigorous
code is permitted, unless to those who shall take an
oath prescribed by 13 and 14 George III. Now if this
is not picking the plums out of the pudding and leaving the mere batter to the Catholics, I know not what is.
If it were merely the Privy Council, it would be (I
allow) nothing but a point of honour for which the mass
of Catholics were contending, the honour of being chief-
mourners or pall-bearers to the country; but surely no
man will contend that every barrister may not specu-
late upon the possibility of being a Puisne Judge; and
that every shopkeeper must not feel himself injured by
his exclusion from borough offices.

One of the greatest practical evils which the Catholics
suffer in Ireland is their exclusion from the offices of
Sheriff and Deputy Sheriff. Nobody who is unac-
quainted with Ireland can conceive the obstacles which
this opposes to the fair administration of justice. The
formation of juries is now entirely in the hands of the
Protestants; the lives, liberties, and properties of the
Catholics in the hands of the juries; and this is the
arrangement for the administration of justice in a
country where religious prejudices are inflamed to the
greatest degree of animosity! In this country, if a man
be a foreigner, if he sell slippers, and sealing wax, and

artificial flowers, we are so tender of human life that
we take care half the number of persons who are to
decide upon his fate should be men of similar prejudices
and feelings with himself : but a poor Catholic in Ireland may be tried by twelve Percevals, and destroyed
according to the manner of that gentleman in the name
of the Lord, and with all the insulting forms of justice.
I do not go the length of saying that deliberate and
wilful injustice is done. I have no doubt that the
Orange Deputy Sheriff thinks it would be a most un-
pardonable breach of his duty if he did not summon a
Protestant panel. I can easily believe that the Protestant panel may conduct themselves very conscientiously in hanging the gentlemen of the crucifix ; but
I blame the law which does not guard the Catholic
against the probable tenor of those feelings which must
unconsciously influence the judgments of mankind.
I detest that state of society which extends unequal
degrees of protection to different creeds and persuasions;
and I cannot describe to you the contempt I feel for a
man who, calling himself a statesman, defends a system
which fills the heart of every Irishman with treason,
and makes his allegiance prudence, not choice.

I request to know if the vestry taxes in Ireland are
a mere matter of romantic feeling which can affect
only the Earl of Fingal ? In a parish where there are
four thousand Catholics and fifty Protestants, the Protestants may meet together in a vestry meeting at which
no Catholic has the right to vote, and tax all the lands
in the parish 1s. 6d. per acre, or in the pound, I forget
which, for the repairs of the church—and how has the

necessity of these repairs been ascertained? A Protestant plumber has discovered that it wants new leading; a Protestant carpenter is convinced the timbers are not sound; and the glazier who hates holy water (as an accoucheur hates celibacy, because he gets not'.ing by it) is employed to put in new sashes.

The grand juries in Ireland are the great scene of jobbing. They have a power of making a county rate to a considerable extent for roads, bridges, and other objects of general accommodation. "You suffer the road to be brought through my park, and I will have the bridge constructed in a situation where it will make a beautiful object to your house. You do my job, and I will do yours." These are the sweet and interesting subjects which occasionally occupy Milesian gentlemen while they are attendant upon this grand inquest of justice. But there is a religion, it seems, even in jobs; and it will be highly gratifying to Mr. Perceval to learn that no man in Ireland who believes in seven sacraments can carry a public road, or bridge, one yard out of the direction most beneficial to the public, and that nobody can cheat the public who does not expound the Scriptures in the purest and most orthodox manner. This will give pleasure to Mr. Perceval: but, from his unfairness upon these topics I appeal to the justice and the proper feelings of Mr. Huskisson. I ask him if the human mind can experience a more dreadful sensation than to see its own jobs refused, and the jobs of another religion perpetually succeeding? I ask him his opinion of a jobless faith, of a creed which dooms a man through

life to a lean and plunderless integrity. He knows
that human nature cannot and will not bear it; and if
we were to paint a political Tartarus, it would be an
endless series of snug expectations and cruel dis-
appointments. These are a few of many dreadful
inconveniences which the Catholics of all ranks suffer
from the laws by which they are at present oppressed.
Besides, look at human nature : what is the history of
all professions ? Joel is to be brought up to the bar :
has Mrs. Plymley the slightest doubt of his being
Chancellor ? Do not his two shrivelled aunts live in
the certainty of seeing him in that situation, and of
cutting out with their own hands his equity habili-
ments ? And I could name a certain minister of the
Gospel who does not, in the bottom of his heart, much
differ from these opinions. Do you think that tho
fathers and mothers of the holy Catholic Church are
not as absurd as Protestant papas and mammas ? The
probability I admit to be, in each particular case, that
the sweet little blockhead will in fact never get a
brief ;—but I will venture to say, there is not a parent
from the Giant's Causeway to Bantry Bay who does
not conceive that his child is the unfortunate victim of
the exclusion, and that nothing short of positive law
could prevent his own dear, pre-eminent Paddy from
rising to the highest honours of the State. So with
the army and parliament ; in fact, few are excluded ;
but, in imagination, all : you keep twenty or thirty
Catholics out, and you lose the affections of four
millions ; and, let me tell you, that recent circumstances
have by no means tended to diminish in the minds of

men that hope of elevation beyond their own rank
which is so congenial to our nature: from pleading for
John Roe to taxing John Bull, from jesting for Mr.
Pitt and writing in the *Anti-Jacobin*, to managing the
affairs of Europe—these are leaps which seem to
justify the fondest dreams of mothers and of aunts.

I do not say that the disabilities to which the
Catholics are exposed amount to such intolerable
grievances, that the strength and industry of a nation
are overwhelmed by them: the increasing prosperity
of Ireland fully demonstrates to the contrary. But I
repeat again, what I have often stated in the course of
our correspondence, that your laws against the Catholics are exactly in that state in which you have neither
the benefits of rigour nor of liberality: every law
which prevented the Catholic from gaining strength
and wealth is repealed; every law which can irritate
remains; if you were determined to insult the Catholics,
you should have kept them weak; if you resolved to
give them strength, you should have ceased to insult
them—at present your conduct is pure, unadulterated
folly.

Lord Hawkesbury says, "We heard nothing about
the Catholics till we began to mitigate the laws
against them; when we relieved them in part from
this oppression they began to be disaffected. This is
very true; but it proves just what I have said, that
you have either done too much or too little; and as
there lives not, I hope, upon earth, so depraved a
courtier that he would load the Catholics with their
ancient chains, what absurdity it is, then, not to

render their dispositions friendly, when you leave their arms and legs free !

You know, and many Englishmen know, what passes in China ; but nobody knows or cares what passes in Ireland. At the beginning of the present reign no Catholic could realise property, or carry on any business ; they were absolutely annihilated, and had no more agency in the country than so many trees. They were like Lord Mulgrave's eloquence and Lord Camden's wit; the legislative bodies did not know of their existence. For these twenty-five years last past the Catholics have been engaged in commerce; within that period the commerce of Ireland has doubled— there are four Catholics at work for one Protestant, and eight Catholics at work for one Episcopalian. Of course, the proportion which Catholic wealth bears to Protestant wealth is every year altering rapidly in favour of the Catholics. I have already told you what their purchases of land were the last year : since that period I have been at some pains to find out the actual state of the Catholic wealth : it is impossible upon such a subject to arrive at complete accuracy; but I have good reason to believe that there are at present 2,000 Catholics in Ireland, possessing an income of £500 and upwards, many of these with incomes of one, two, three, and four thousand, and some amounting to fifteen and twenty thousand per annum :—and this is the kingdom, and these the people, for whose concilia- tion we are to wait Heaven knows when, and Lord Hawkesbury why ! As for me, I never think of the situation of Ireland without feeling the same necessity

for immediate interference as I should do if I saw
blood flowing from a great artery. I rush towards it
with the instinctive rapidity of a man desirous of preventing death, and have no other feeling but that in a
few seconds the patient may be no more.

I could not help smiling, in the times of No Popery,
to witness the loyal indignation of many persons at
the attempt made by the last ministry to do something
for the relief of Ireland. The general cry in the
country was, that they would not see their beloved
Monarch used ill in his old age, and that they would
stand by him to the last drop of their blood. I
respect good feelings, however erroneous be the occasions on which they display themselves; and therefore
I saw in all this as much to admire as to blame. It
was a species of affection, however, which reminded
me very forcibly of the attachment displayed by the
servants of the Russian ambassador at the beginning
of the last century. His Excellency happened to fall
down in a kind of apoplectic fit, when he was paying a
morning visit in the house of an acquaintance. The
confusion was of course very great, and messengers
were despatched in every direction to find a surgeon :
who, upon his arrival, declared that his Excellency
must be immediately blooded, and prepared himself
forthwith to perform the operation : the barbarous
servants of the embassy, who were there in great
numbers, no sooner saw the surgeon prepared to wound
the arm of their master with a sharp, shining instrument, than they drew their swords, put themselves in
an attitude of defence, and swore in pure Sclavonic,

"that they would murder any man who attempted to do him the slightest injury: he had been a very good master to them, and they would not desert him in his misfortunes, or suffer his blood to be shed while he was off his guard, and incapable of defending himself." By good fortune, the secretary arrived about this period of the dispute, and his Excellency, relieved from superfluous blood and perilous affection, was, after much difficulty, restored to life.

There is an argument brought forward with some appearance of plausibility in the House of Commons, which certainly merits an answer: You know that the Catholics now vote for members of parliament in Ireland, and that they outnumber the Protestants in a very great proportion; if you allow Catholics to sit in parliament, religion will be found to influence votes more than property, and the greater part of the 100 Irish members who are returned to parliament will be Catholics. Add to these the Catholic members who are returned in England, and you will have a phalanx of heretical strength which every minister will be compelled to respect, and occasionally to conciliate by concessions incompatible with the interests of the Protestant Church. The fact is, however, that you are at this moment subjected to every danger of this kind which you can possibly apprehend hereafter. If the spiritual interests of the voters are more powerful than their temporal interests, they can bind down their representatives to support any measures favourable to the Catholic religion, and they can change the objects of their choice till they have found Protestant

members (as they easily may do) perfectly obedient to
their wishes. If the superior possessions of the Protestants prevent the Catholics from uniting for a
common political object, then the danger you fear
cannot exist: if zeal, on the contrary, gets the better
of acres, then the danger at present exists, from the
right of voting already given to the Catholics, and it
will not be increased by allowing them to sit in parliament. There are, as nearly as I can recollect,
thirty seats in Ireland for cities and counties, where
the Protestants are the most numerous, and where the
members returned must of course be Protestants. In
the other seventy representations the wealth of the
Protestants is opposed to the number of the Catholics;
and if all the seventy members returned were of the
Catholic persuasion, they must still plot the destruction of our religion in the midst of 588 Protestants.
Such terrors would disgrace a cook-maid, or a toothless
aunt—when they fall from the lips of bearded and
senatorial men, they are nauseous, antiperistaltic, and
emetical.

How can you for a moment doubt of the rapid effects
which would be produced by the emancipation? In
the first place, to my certain knowledge the Catholics
have long since expressed to his Majesty's Ministers
their perfect readiness *to rest in his Majesty, either
with the consent of the Pope, or without it if it cannot
be obtained, the nomination of the Catholic prelacy.*
The Catholic prelacy in Ireland consists of twenty-six
bishops and the warden of Galway, a dignitary enjoying
Catholic jurisdiction. The number of Roman Catholic

priests in Ireland exceeds one thousand. The expenses of his peculiar worship are, to a substantial farmer or mechanic, five shillings per annum; to a labourer (where he is not entirely excused) one shilling per annum; this includes the contribution of the whole family, and for this the priest is bound to attend them when sick, and to confess them when they apply to him; he is also to keep his chapel in order, to celebrate divine service, and to preach on Sundays and holydays. In the northern district a priest gains from £30 to £50; in the other parts of Ireland from £60 to £90 per annum. The best paid Catholic bishops receive about £400 per annum; the others from £300 to £350. My plan is very simple: I would have 300 Catholic parishes at £100 per annum, 300 at £200 per annum, and 400 at £300 per annum; this, for the whole thousand parishes, would amount to £190,000. To the prelacy I would allot £20,000 in unequal proportions, from £1,000 to £500; and I would appropriate £40,000 more for the support of Catholic schools, and the repairs of Catholic churches; the whole amount of which sum is £250,000, about the expense of three days of one of our genuine, good English *just and necessary wars*. The clergy should all receive their salaries at the Bank of Ireland, and I would place the whole patronage in the hands of the Crown. Now, I appeal to any human being, except Spencer Perceval, Esq., of the parish of Hampstead, what the disaffection of a clergy would amount to, gaping after this graduated bounty of the Crown, and whether Ignatius Loyala himself, if he were a living blockhead instead of a dead saint, could

withstand the temptation of bouncing from £100 a year
at Sligo, to £300 in Tipperary? This is the miserable
sum of money for which the merchants and landowners
and nobility of England are exposing themselves to
the tremendous peril of losing Ireland. The sinecure
places of the Roses and the Percevals, and the "dear
and near relations," put up to auction at thirty years'
purchase, would almost amount to the money.

I admit that nothing can be more reasonable than to
expect that a Catholic priest should starve to death,
genteelly and pleasantly, for the good of the Protestant
religion ; but is it equally reasonable to expect that he
should do so for the Protestant pews, and Protestant brick and mortar? On an Irish Sabbath, the
bell of a neat parish church often summons to church
only the parson and an occasionally conforming clerk;
while, two hundred yards off, a thousand Catholics are
huddled together in a miserable hovel, and pelted by
all the storms of heaven. Can anything be more dis-
tressing than to see a venerable man pouring forth
sublime truths in tattered breeches, and depending for
his food upon the little offal he gets from his parish-
ioners? I venerate a human being who starves for
his principles, let them be what they may; but starving
for anything is not at all to the taste of the honourable
flagellants: strict principles, and good pay, is the motto
of Mr. Perceval: the one he keeps in great measure
for the faults of his enemies, the other for himself.

There are parishes in Connaught in which a Protestant was never settled nor even seen. In that province
in Munster, and in parts of Leinster, the entire pea-

santry for sixty miles are Catholics ; in these tracts the churches are frequently shut for want of a congregation, or opened to an assemblage of from six to twenty persons. Of what Protestants there are in Ireland, the greatest part are gathered together in Ulster, or they live in towns. In the country of the other three provinces the Catholics see no other religion but their own, and are at the least as fifteen to one Protestant. In the diocese of Tuam they are sixty to one; in the parish of St. Mulins, diocese of Leghlin, there are four thousand Catholics and one Protestant ; in the town of Grasgenamana, in the county of Kilkenny, there are between four and five hundred Catholic houses, and three Protestant houses. In the parish of Allen, county Kildare, there is no Protestant, though it is very populous. In the parish of Arlesin, Queen's County, the proportion is one hundred to one. In the whole county of Kilkenny, by actual enumeration, it is seventeen to one ; in the diocese of Kilmacduagh, province of Connaught, fifty-two to one, by ditto. These I give you as a few specimens of the present state of Ireland ; and yet there are men impudent and ignorant enough to contend that such evils require no remedy, and that mild family man who dwelleth in Hampstead can find none but the cautery and the knife.

> ———" Omne per ignem
> Excoquitur vitium."

I cannot describe the horror and disgust which I felt at hearing Mr. Perceval call upon the then Ministry for measures of vigour in Ireland. If I lived at Hampstead upon stewed meats and claret; if I walked to church every Sunday before eleven young gentlemen of my own begetting, with their faces washed, and their hair pleasingly combed ; if the Almighty had blessed me with every earthly comfort—how awfully would I pause before I sent forth the flame and the sword over the cabins of the poor, brave, generous, open-hearted peasants of Ireland! How easy it is to shed human blood; how easy it is to persuade ourselves that it is our duty to do so, and that the decision has cost us a severe struggle; how much in all ages have wounds and shrieks and tears been the cheap and vulgar resources of the rulers of mankind ; how difficult and how noble it is to govern in kindness and to found an empire upon the everlasting basis of justice and affection! But what do men call vigour ? To let loose hussars and to bring up artillery, to govern with lighted matches, and to cut, and push, and prime ; I call this not vigour, but the *sloth of cruelty and ignorance.* The vigour I love consists in finding out wherein subjects are aggrieved, in relieving them, in studying the temper and genius of a people, in consulting their prejudices, in selecting proper persons to lead and manage them, in the laborious, watchful, and difficult task of increasing public happiness by allaying each particular discontent. In this way Hoche pacified La Vendée—and in this way only will Ireland ever be subdued. But this, in the eyes of Mr. Perceval, is imbecility and meanness. Houses are not broken open, women are not insulted, the people seem all to be happy ; they are not rode over by horses, and cut by whips. Do you call this vigour? Is this government?

LETTER X. AND LAST.

You must observe that all I have said of the effects which will be produced by giving salaries to the Catholic clergy, only proceeds upon the supposition that the emanciptaion of the laity is effected :—without that, I am sure there is not a clergyman in Ireland who would receive a shilling from government; he could not do so, without an entire loss of credit among the members of his own persuasion.

What you say of the moderation of the Irish Protestant clergy in collecting tithes, is, I believe, strictly true. Instead of collecting what the law enables them to collect, I believe they seldom or ever collect more than two-thirds; and I entirely agree with you, that the abolition of agistment tithe in Ireland by a vote of the Irish House of Commons, and without any remuneration to the Church, was a most scandalous and Jacobinical measure. I do not blame the Irish clergy; but I submit to your common sense, if it be possible to explain to an Irish peasant upon what principle of justice, or common sense, he is to pay every tenth potato in his little garden to a clergyman in whose religion nobody believes for twenty miles around him, and who has nothing to preach to but bare walls ? It is true, if the tithes are bought up, the cottager must pay more rent to his landlord; but the same thing done in the shape of rent is less odious than when it is done in the shape of tithe. I do not want to take a shilling out of the pockets of the clergy, but to leave the substance of things, and to change their names. I cannot see the slightest reason why the Irish labourer is to be relieved from the real onus, or from anything else but the name of tithe. At present he rents only nine-tenths of the produce of the land, which is all that belongs to the owner; this he has at the market price; if the landowner purchase the other tenth of the Church, of course he has a right to make a correspondent advance upon his tenant.

I very much doubt, if you were to lay open all civil offices to the Catholics, and to grant salaries to their clergy, in the manner I have stated, if the Catholic laity would give themselves much trouble about the advance of their Church; for they would pay the same tithes under one system that they do under another. If you were to bring the Catholics into the daylight of the world, to the high situations of the army, the navy, and the bar, numbers of them would come over to the Established Church, and do as other people do; instead of that, you set a mark of infamy upon them, rouse every passion of our nature in favour of their creed, and then wonder that men are blind to the follies of the Catholic religion. There are hardly any instances of old and rich families among the Protestant Dissenters: when a man keeps a coach, and lives in good company, he comes to church, and gets ashamed of the meeting-house; if this is not the case with the father, it is almost always the case with the son. These things would never be so if the Dissenters were in *practice* as much excluded from all the concerns of civil life as the Catholics are. If a rich young Catholic were in Parliament, he would belong to White's and to Brookes's,

would keep race-horses, would walk up and down Pall
Mall, be exonerated of his ready money and his constitution, become as totally devoid of morality, honesty,
knowledge, and civility as Protestant loungers in Pall
Mall, and return home with a supreme contempt for
Father O'Leary and Father O'Callaghan.   I am
astonished at the madness of the Catholic clergy in not
perceiving that Catholic emancipation is Catholic infidelity; that to entangle their people in the intrigues
of a Protestant parliament, and a Protestant court, is to
ensure the loss of every man of fashion and consequence
in their community.   The true receipt for preserving
their religion, is Mr. Perceval's receipt for destroying
it: it is to deprive every rich Catholic of all the
objects of secular ambition, to separate him from the
Protestant, and to shut him up in his castle with priests
and relics.   *

We are told, in answer to all our arguments, that
this is not a fit period—that a period of universal war
is not the proper time for dangerous innovations in the
constitution: this is as much as to say, that the worst
time for making friends is the period when you have
made many enemies; that it is the greatest of all errors
to stop when you are breathless, and to lie down when
you are fatigued.   Of one thing I am quite certain: if
the safety of Europe is once completely restored, the
Catholics may for ever bid adieu to the slightest probability of effecting their object.   Such men as hang
about a court not only are deaf to the suggestions of
mere justice, but they despise justice; they detest the
word *right*; the only word which rouses them is *peril*;

where they can oppress with impunity, they oppress for ever, and call it loyalty and wisdom.

I am so far from conceiving the legitimate strength of the Crown would be diminished by these abolitions of civil incapacities in consequence of religious opinions, that my only objection to the increase of religious freedom is, that it would operate as a diminution of political freedom ; the power of the Crown is so over-bearing at this period, that almost the only steady opposers of its fatal influence are men disgusted by religious intolerance. Our establishments are so enor-mous, and so utterly disproportioned to our population, that every second or third man you meet in society gains something from the public ; my brother the com-missioner,—my nephew the police justice,—purveyor of small beer to the army in Ireland,—clerk of the mouth,—yeoman to the left hand,—these are the obstacles which common sense and justice have now to overcome. Add to this that the King, old and infirm, excites a principle of very amiable generosity in his favour ; that he has led a good, moral, and religious life, equally removed from profligacy and methodistical hypocrisy ; that he has been a good husband, a good father, and a good master ; that he dresses plain, loves hunting and farming, hates the French, and is in all his opinions and habits, quite English :—these feelings are heightened by the present situation of the world, and the yet unexploded clamour of Jacobinism. In short, from the various sources of interest, personal regard, and national taste, such a tempest of loyalty has set in upon the people that the 47th proposition in Euclid might now be voted down with as much ease as any proposition in politics; and therefore if Lord Hawkesbury hates the abstract truths of science as much as he hates concrete truth in human affairs, now is his time for getting rid of the multiplication table, and passing a vote of censure upon the pretensions of the *hypotenuse*. Such is the history of English parties at this moment : you cannot seriously suppose that the people care for such men as Lord Hawkesbury, Mr. Canning, and Mr. Perceval on their own account; you cannot really believe them to be so degraded as to look to their safety from a man who proposes to subdue Europe by keeping it without Jesuit's Bark. The people at present have one passion, and but one—

"A Jove principium, Jovis omnia plena."

They care no more for the ministers I have mentioned, than they do for those sturdy royalists who for £60 per annum stand behind his Majesty's carriage, arrayed in scarlet and in gold. If the present ministers opposed the Court instead of flattering it, they would not command twenty votes.

Do not imagine by these observations that I am not loyal; without joining in the common cant of the best of kings, I respect the King most sincerely as a good man. His religion is better than the religion of Mr. Perceval, his old morality very superior to the old morality of Mr. Canning, and I am quite certain he has a safer understanding than both of them put together. Loyalty within the bounds of reason and moderation is one of the great instruments of human happiness; but the love of the king may easily become more strong than the love of the kingdom, and we may lose sight of the public welfare in our exaggerated admiration of him who is appointed to reign only for its promotion and support. I detest Jacobinism; and if I am doomed to be a slave at all, I would rather be the slave of a king than a cobbler. God save the King, you say, warms your heart like the sound of a trumpet. I cannot make use of so violent a metaphor; but I am delighted to hear it, when it is the cry of genuine affection; I am delighted to hear it when they hail not only the individual man, but the outward and living sign of all English blessings. These are noble feelings, and the heart of every good man must go with them; but God save the King, in these times, too often means God save my pension and my place, God give my sisters an allowance out of the privy purse—make me clerk of the irons, let me survey the meltings, let me live upon the fruits of other men's industry, and fatten upon the plunder of the public.

What is it possible to say to such a man as the Gentleman of Hampstead, who really believes it feasible to convert the four million Irish Catholics to the Protestant religion, and considers this as the best remedy for the disturbed state of Ireland? It is not possible to answer such a man with arguments; we must come out against him with beads and a cowl, and push him into an hermitage. It is really such trash, that it is an abuse of the privilege of reasoning to reply to it. Such a project is well worthy the states-man who would bring the French to reason by keeping them without rhubarb, and exhibit to mankind the awful spectacle of a nation deprived of neutral salts. This is not the dream of a wild apothecary indulging in his own opium; this is not the distempered fancy of a pounder of drugs, delirious from smallness of profits; but it is the sober, deliberate, and systematic scheme of a man to whom the public safety is intrusted, and whose appointment is considered by many as a master-piece of political sagacity. What a sublime thought, that no purge can now be taken between the Weser and the Garonne; that the bustling pestle is still, the canorous mortar mute, and the bowels of mankind locked up for fourteen degrees of latitude! When, I should be curious to know, were all the powers of crudity and flatulence fully explained to his Majesty's ministers? At what period was this great plan of conquest and constipation fully developed? In whose mind was the idea of destroying the pride and the plasters of France first engendered? Without castor oil they might for some months, to be sure, have carried on a lingering war! but can they do without bark? Will the people live under a government where antimonial powders cannot be procured? Will they bear the loss of mercury? "There's the rub." Depend upon it, the absence of the materia medica will soon bring them to their senses, and the cry of *Bourbon and bolus* burst forth from the Baltic to the Mediter-ranean.

You ask me for any precedent in our history where the oath of supremacy has been dispensed with. It was dispensed with to the Catholics of Canada in 1774.

They are only required to take a simple oath of allegiance. The same, I believe, was the case in Corsica. The reason of such exemption was obvious; you could not possibly have retained either of these countries without it. And what did it signify, whether you retained them or not? In cases where you might have been foolish without peril you were wise; when nonsense and bigotry threaten you with destruction, it is impossible to bring you back to the alphabet of justice and common sense. If men are to be fools, I would rather they were fools in little matters than in great; dulness turned up with temerity is a livery all the worse for the facings; and the most tremendous of all things is the magnanimity of the dunce.

It is not by any means necessary, as you contend, to repeal the Test Act if you give relief to the Catholic: what the Catholics ask for is to be put on a footing with the Protestant Dissenters, which would be done by repealing that part of the law which compels them to take the oath of supremacy and to make the declaration against transubstantiation: they would then come into Parliament as all other Dissenters are allowed to do, and the penal laws to which they were exposed for taking office would be suspended every year, as they have been for this half century past towards Protestant Dissenters. Perhaps, after all, this is the best method —to continue the persecuting law, and to suspend it every year—a method which, while it effectually destroys the persecution itself, leaves to the great mass of mankind the exquisite gratification of supposing that they are enjoying some advantage from which a particular class of their fellow creatures are excluded. We manage the Corporation and Test Acts at present much in the same manner as if we were to persuade parish boys who had been in the habit of beating an ass to spare the animal, and beat the skin of an ass stuffed with straw; this would preserve the semblance of tormenting without the reality, and keep boy and beast in good humour.

How can you imagine that a provision for the Catholic clergy affects the 5th article of the Union? Surely I am preserving the Protestant Church in Ireland if I put it in a better condition than that in which it now is. A tithe proctor in Ireland collects his tithes with a blunderbuss, and carries his tenth hay-cock by storm, sword in hand: to give him equal value in a more pacific shape cannot, I should imagine, be considered as injurious to the Church of Ireland; and what right has that Church to complain if Parliament chooses to fix upon the empire the burden of supporting a double ecclesiastical establishment? Are the revenues of the Irish Protestant clergy in the slightest degree injured by such provision? On the contrary, is it possible to confer a more serious benefit upon that Church than by quieting and contenting those who are at work for its destruction?

It is impossible to think of the affairs of Ireland without being forcibly struck with the parallel of Hungary. Of her seven millions of inhabitants, one half were Protestants, Calvinists, and Lutherans, many of the Greek Church, and many Jews: such was the state of their religious dissensions that Mahomet had often been called in to the aid of Calvin, and the crescent often glittered on the walls of Buda and Pres- burg. At last, in 1791, during the most violent crisis of disturbance, a Diet was called, and by a great majority of voices a decree was passed, which secured to all the contending sects the fullest and freest exer- cise of religious worship and education; ordained—let it be heard in Hampstead—that churches and chapels should be erected for all on the most perfectly equal terms; that the Protestants of both confessions should depend upon their spiritual superiors alone; liberated them from swearing by the usual oath, "the Holy Vir- gin Mary, the saints, and chosen of God;" and then the decree adds, "that *public offices and honours, high or low, great or small, shall be given to natural-born Hungarians who deserve well of their country, and possess the other qualifications, let their religion be what it may.*" Such was the line of policy pursued in a Diet consisting of four hundred members, in a state whose form of government approaches nearer to our own than any other, having a Roman Catholic estab- lishment of great wealth and power, and under the influence of one of the most bigoted Catholic Courts in Europe. This measure has now the experience of eighteen years in its favour; it has undergone a trial of fourteen years of revolution such as the world never witnessed, and more than equal to a century less convulsed: What have been its effects? When the French advanced like a torrent within a few days' march of Vienna, the Hungarians rose in a mass; they formed what they called the sacred insurrection, to defend their sovereign, their rights and liberties, now common to all; and the apprehension of their approach dictated to the reluctant Bonaparte the immediate signature of the treaty of *Leoben.* The Romish hierarchy of Hungary exists in all its former splendour and opulence; never has the slightest attempt been made to diminish it; and those revolutionary principles, to which so large a portion of civilised Europe has been sacrificed, have here failed in making the smallest successful inroad.

The whole history of this proceeding of the Hungarian Diet is so extraordinary, and such an admirable comment upon the Protestantism of Mr. Spencer Perceval, that I must compel you to read a few short extracts from the law itself :—" The Protestants of both confessions shall, in religious matters, depend upon their own spiritual superiors alone. The Protestants may likewise retain their trivial and grammar schools. The Church dues which the Protestants have hitherto paid to the Catholic parish priests, schoolmasters, or other such officers, either in money, productions, or labour, shall in future entirely cease, and after three months from the publishing of this law, be no more anywhere demanded. In the building or repairing of churches, parsonage-houses, and schools, the Protestants are not obliged to assist the Catholics with labour, nor the Catholics the Protestants. The pious foundations and donations of the Protestants which already exist, or which in future may be made for their churches, ministers, schools and students, hospitals, orphan houses, and poor, cannot be taken from them

under any pretext, nor yet the care of them; but rather
the unimpeded administration shall be intrusted to those
from among them to whom it legally belongs, and those
foundations which may have been taken from them
under the last government shall be returned to them
without delay. All affairs of marriage of the Protestants are left to their own consistories; all landlords
and masters of families, under the penalty of public
prosecution, are ordered not to prevent their subjects
and servants, whether they be Catholic or Protestant,
from the observance of the festivals and ceremonies of
their religion," etc. etc. etc.—By what strange chances
are mankind influenced! A little Catholic barrister of
Vienna might have raised the cry of *No Protestantism*,
and Hungary would have panted for the arrival of a
French army as much as Ireland does at this moment;
arms would have been searched for; Lutheran and Cal-
vinist houses entered in the dead of the night; and the
strength of Austria exhausted in guarding a country
from which, under the present liberal system, she may
expect in the moment of danger the most powerful aid:
and let it be remembered that this memorable example
of political wisdom took place at a period when many
great monarchies were yet unconquered in Europe; in
a country where the two religious parties were equal in
number; and where it is impossible to suppose indifference in the party which relinquished its exclusive privileges. Under all these circumstances the measure
was carried in the Hungarian Diet by a majority of
280 to 120. In a few weeks we shall see every concession denied to the Catholics by a much larger

majority of Protestants, at a moment when every other power is subjugated but ourselves, and in a country where the oppressed are four times as numerous as their oppressors.   So much for the wisdom of our ancestors— so much for the nineteenth century—so much for the superiority of the English over all the nations of the Continent.

Are you not sensible, let me ask you, of the absurdity of trusting the lowest Catholics with offices correspondent to their situation in life, and of denying such privileges to the highei ?   A Catholic may serve in the militia, but a Catholic cannot come into Parliament; in the latter case you suspect combination, and in the former case you suspect no combination; you deliberately arm ten or twenty thousand of the lowest of the Catholic people; and the moment you come to a class of men whose education, honour, and talents seem to render all mischief less probable, then you see the danger of employing a Catholic, and cling to your investigating tests and disabling laws.   If you tell me you have enough of members of Parliament and not enough of militia without the Catholics, I beg leave to remind you that, by employing the physical force of any sect at the same time when you leave them in a state of utter disaffection, you are not adding strength to your armies, but weakness and ruin.   If you want the vigour of their common people, you must not disgrace their nobility and insult their priesthood.

I thought that the terror of the Pope had been confined to the limits of the nursery, and merely employed as a means to induce young master to enter into his

small-clothes with greater speed and to eat his breakfast with greater attention to decorum. For these
purposes the name of the Pope is admirable; but why
push it beyond? Why not leave to Lord Hawkesbury
all further enumeration of the Pope's powers? For a
whole century you have been exposed to the enmity of
France, and your succession was disputed in two rebellions: what could the Pope do at the period when there
was a serious struggle whether England should be Protestant or Catholic, and when the issue was completely
doubtful? Could the Pope induce the Irish to rise in
1715? Could he induce them to rise in 1745? You
had no Catholic enemy when half this island was in
arms; and what did the Pope attempt in the last rebellion in Ireland? But if he had as much power over
the minds of the Irish as Mr. Wilberforce has over the
mind of a young Methodist converted the preceding
quarter, is this a reason why we are to disgust men who
may be acted upon in such a manner by a foreign
power? or is it not an additional reason why we should
raise up every barrier of affection and kindness against
the mischief of foreign influence? But the true answer
is, the mischief does not exist. Gog and Magog have
produced as much influence upon human affairs as the
Pope has done for this half century past; and by spoiling him of his possessions, and degrading him in the
eyes of all Europe, Bonaparte has not taken quite the
proper method of increasing his influence.

But why not a Catholic king as well as a Catholic
member of Parliament, or of the Cabinet?—Because it
is probable that the one would be mischievous and the

other not. A Catholic king might struggle against the Protestantism of the country, and if the struggle were not successful it would at least be dangerous; but the efforts of any other Catholic would be quite insignificant, and his hope of success so small, that it is quite improbable the effort would ever be made: my argument is, that in so Protestant a country as Great Britain, the character of her parliaments and her cabinet could not be changed by the few Catholics who would ever find their way to the one or the other. But the power of the Crown is immeasurably greater than the power which the Catholics could obtain from any other species of authority in the state; and it does not follow because the lesser degree of power is innocent that the greater should be so too. As for the stress you lay upon the danger of a Catholic chancellor, I have not the least hesitation in saying that his appointment would not do a ten thousandth part of the mischief to the English Church that might be done by a Methodistical chancellor of the true Clapham breed; and I request to know if it is really so very necessary that a chancellor should be of the religion of the Church of England, how many chancellors you have had within the last century who have been bred up in the Presbyterian religion? And again, how many you have had who notoriously have been without any religion at all?

Why are you to suppose that eligibility and election are the same thing, and that all the cabinet *will* be Catholics whenever all the cabinet *may* be Catholics? You have a right, you say, to suppose an extreme case,

and to argue upon it—so have I: and I will suppose
that the hundred Irish members will one day come
down in a body and pass a law compelling the King to
reside in Dublin. I will suppose that the Scotch members, by a similar stratagem, will lay England under a
large contribution of meal and sulphur: no measure is
without objection if you sweep the whole horizon for
danger; it is not sufficient to tell me of what may
happen, but you must show me a rational probability
that it will happen: after all, I might, contrary to my
real opinion, admit all your dangers to exist; it is
enough for me to contend that all other dangers taken
together are not equal to the danger of losing Ireland
from disaffection and invasion.

I am astonished to see you, and many good and well-
meaning clergymen beside you, painting the Catholics
in such detestable colours; two-thirds, at least, of
Europe are Catholics—they are Christians, though
mistaken Christians; how can I possibly admit that
any sect of Christians, and, above all, that the oldest
and the most numerous sect of Christians are incapable
of fulfilling the common duties and relations of life:
though I do differ from them in many particulars, God
forbid I should give such a handle to infidelity, and
subscribe to such blasphemy against our common
religion?

Do you think mankind never change their opinions
without formally expressing and confessing that
change? When you quote the decisions of ancient
Catholic councils, are you prepared to defend all
the decrees of English convocations and universities

since the reign of Queen Elizabeth? I could soon make you sick of your uncandid industry against the Catholics, and bring you to allow that it is better to forget times past, and to judge and be judged by present opinions and present practice.

I must beg to be excused from explaining and refuting all the mistakes about the Catholics made by my Lord Redesdale; and I must do that nobleman the justice to say, that he has been treated with great disrespect. Could anything be more indecent than to make it a morning lounge in Dublin to call upon his Lordship, and to cram him with Arabian-night stories about the Catholics? Is this proper behaviour to the representative of Majesty, the child of Themis, and the keeper of the conscience in West Britain? Whoever reads the Letters of the Catholic Bishops, in the appendix to Sir John Hippesly's very sensible book, will see to what an excess this practice must have been carried with the pleasing and Protestant nobleman whose name I have mentioned, and from thence I wish you to receive your answer about excommunication, and all the trash which is talked against the Catholics.

A sort of notion has, by some means or another, crept into the world that difference of religion would render men unfit to perform together the offices of common and civil life : that Brother Wood and Brother Grose could not travel together the same circuit if they differed in creed, nor Cockell and Mingay be engaged in the same cause, if Cockell was a Catholic and Mingay a Muggletonian. It is supposed that

Huskisson and Sir Harry Englefield would squabble
behind the Speaker's chair about the council of Lateran,
and many a turnpike bill miscarry by the sarcastical
controversies of Mr. Hawkins Brown and Sir John
Throckmorton upon the real presence. I wish I could
see some of these symptoms of earnestness upon the
subject of religion; but it really seems to me that, in
the present state of society, men no more think about
inquiring concerning each other's faith than they do
concerning the colour of each other's skins. There
may have been times in England when the quarter
sessions would have been disturbed by theological
polemics; but now, after a Catholic justice had once
been seen on the bench, and it had been clearly
ascertained that he spoke English, had no tail, only a
single row of teeth, and that he loved port wine—
after all the scandalous and infamous reports of his
physical conformation had been clearly proved to be
false—he would be reckoned a jolly fellow, and very
superior in flavour to a sly Presbyterian. Nothing, in
fact, can be more uncandid and unphilosophical than to
say that a man has a tail, because you cannot agree with
him upon religious subjects; it appears to be ludicrous:
but I am convinced it has done infinite mischief to
the Catholics, and made a very serious impression
upon the minds of many gentlemen of large landed
property.

In talking of the impossibility of Catholic and Protestant living together with equal privilege under the
same government, do you forget the Cantons of
Switzerland? You might have seen there a Protes-

taut congregation going into a church which had just been quitted by a Catholic congregation; and I will venture to say that the Swiss Catholics were more bigoted to their religion than any people in the whole world. Did the kings of Prussia ever refuse to employ a Catholic? Would Frederick the Great have rejected an able man on this account? We have seen Prince Czartorinski, a Catholic Secretary of State in Russia; in former times a Greek patriarch and an apostolic vicar acted together in the most perfect harmony in Venice; and we have seen the Emperor of Germany in modern times intrusting the care of his person and the command of his guard to a Protestant Prince, Frederick of Wittemberg. But what are all these things to Mr. Perceval? He has looked at human nature from the top of Hampstead Hill, and has not a thought beyond the little sphere of his own vision. "The snail," say the Hindoos, "sees nothing but his own shell, and thinks it the grandest palace in the universe."

I now take a final leave of this subject of Ireland; the only difficulty in discussing it is a want of resistance, a want of something difficult to unravel, and something dark to illumine. To agitate such a question is to beat the air with a club, and cut down gnats with a scimitar; it is a prostitution of industry, and a waste of strength. If a man say, I have a good place, and I do not choose to lose it, this mode of arguing upon the Catholic question I can well understand; but that any human being with an understanding two degrees elevated above that of an Anabaptist preacher, should conscientiously contend for the expediency and propriety of leaving the Irish Catholics in their present state, and of subjecting us to such tremendous peril in the present condition of the world, it is utterly out of my power to conceive. Such a measure as the Catholic question is entirely beyond the common game of politics; it is a measure in which all parties ought to acquiesce, in order to preserve the place where and the stake for which they play. If Ireland is gone, where are jobs? where are reversions? where is my brother Lord Arden? where are my dear and near relations? The game is up, and the Speaker of the House of Commons will be sent as a present to the menagerie at Paris. We talk of waiting from particular considerations, as if centuries of joy and prosperity were before us : in the next ten years our fate must be decided; we shall know, long before that period, whether we can bear up against the miseries by which we are threatened or not ; and yet, in the very midst of our crisis, we are enjoined to abstain from the most certain means of increasing our strength, and advised to wait for the remedy till the disease is removed by death or health. And now, instead of the plain and manly policy of increasing unanimity at home, by equalising rights and privileges, what is the ignorant, arrogant, and wicked system which has been pursued? Such a career of madness and of folly was, I believe, never run in so short a period. The vigour of the ministry is like the vigour of a grave-digger—the tomb becomes more ready and more wide for every effort which they make. There is nothing which it is worth while either to take or to retain, and a constant train of ruinous expeditions have been kept up. Every Englishman felt proud of the integrity of his country; the character of the country is lost for ever. It is of the utmost consequence to a commercial people at war with the greatest part of Europe, that there should be a free entry of neutrals into the enemy's ports; the neutrals who carried our manufactures we have not only excluded, but we have compelled them to declare war against us. It was our interest to make a good peace, or convince our own people that it could not be obtained; we have not made a peace, and we have convinced the people of nothing but of the arrogance of the Foreign Secretary : and all this has taken place in the short space of a year, because a King's Bench barrister and a writer of epigrams, turned into Ministers of State, were determined to show country gentlemen that the late administration had no vigour. In the meantime commerce stands still, manufactures perish, Ireland is more and more irritated, India is threatened, fresh taxes are accumulated upon the wretched people, the war is carried on without it being possible to conceive any one single object which a rational being can propose to himself by its continuation; and in the midst of this unparalleled insanity we are told that the Continent is to be reconquered by the want of rhubarb and plums. A better spirit than exists in the English people never existed in any people in the world : it has been misdirected, and squandered upon party purposes in the most degrading and scandalous manner; they have been led to believe that they were benefiting the commerce of England by

destroying the commerce of America, that they were
defending their Sovereign by perpetuating the bigoted
oppression of their fellow-subjects; their rulers and
their guides have told them that they would equal the
vigour of France by equalling her atrocity; and they have
gone on wasting that opulence, patience, and courage,
which, if husbanded by prudent and moderate counsels,
might have proved the salvation of mankind. The
same policy of turning the good qualities of Englishmen
to their own destruction, which made Mr. Pitt omnipo-
tent, continues his power to those who resemble him
only in his vices; advantage is taken of the loyalty of
Englishmen to make them meanly submissive; their
piety is turned into persecution, their courage into
useless and obstinate contention; they are plundered
because they are ready to pay, and soothed into asinine
stupidity because they are full of virtuous patience. If
England must perish at last, so let it be : that event is
in the hands of God; we must dry up our tears and
submit. But that England should perish swindling
and stealing; that it should perish waging war against
lazar houses and hospitals; that it should perish persecuting with monastic bigotry; that it should calmly
give itself up to be ruined by the flashy arrogance of
one man, and the narrow fanaticism of another; these
events are within the power of human beings, and I
did not think that the magnanimity of Englishmen
would ever stoop to such degradations.

Longum Vale !

PETER PLYMLEY.

HISTORICAL APOLOGY FOR THE IRISH CATHOLICS.

Historical Apology for the Irish Catholics. By WILLIAM PARNELL, Esquire. Fitzpatrick, Dublin. 1807.

———•◦•———

IF ever a nation exhibited symptoms of downright madness, or utter stupidity, we conceive these symptoms may be easily recognised in the conduct of this country upon the Catholic question. A man has a wound in his great toe, and a violent and perilous fever at the same time; and he refuses to take the medicines for the fever because it will disconcert the toe! The mournful and folly-stricken blockhead forgets that his toe cannot survive him; that if he dies, there can be no digital life apart from him : yet he lingers and fondles over this last part of his body, soothing it madly with little plasters, and anile fomentations, while the neglected fever rages in his entrails, and burns away his whole life. If the comparatively little questions of Establishment are all that this country is capable of discussing or regarding, for God's sake let us remember that the foreign conquest, which destroys all, destroys this beloved *toe* also. Pass over freedom, industry, and science—and look upon this great empire, by which we are about to be

E—46

swallowed up, only as it affects the manner of collecting tithes, and of reading the liturgy—still, if all
goes, these must go too ; and even, for their interests,
it is worth while to conciliate Ireland, to avert the
hostility, and to employ the strength of the Catholic
population. We plead the question as the sincerest
friends to the Establishment ;—as wishing to it all
the prosperity and duration its warmest advocates can
desire,—but remembering always what these advocates
seem to forget, that the Establishment cannot be
threatened by any danger so great as the perdition of
the kingdom in which it is established.

We are truly glad to agree so entirely with Mr.
Parnell upon this great question ; we admire his way
of thinking, and most cordially recommend his work
to the attention of the public. The general conclusion
which he attempts to prove is this : that religious
sentiment, however perverted by bigotry or fanaticism,
has always a *tendency* to moderation ; that it seldom
assumes any great portion of activity or enthusiasm,
except from novelty of opinion, or from opposition,
contumely, and persecution, when novelty ceases ; that
a Government has little to fear from any religious
sect, except while that sect is new. Give a Government only time, and, provided it has the good sense to
treat folly with forbearance, it must ultimately prevail.
When, therefore, a sect is found, after a lapse of years,
to be ill-disposed to the Government, we may be
certain that Government has widened its separation by
marked distinctions, roused its resentment by contumely, or supported its enthusiasm by persecution.

The *particular* conclusion Mr. Parnell attempts to prove is, that the Catholic religion in Ireland had sunk into torpor and inactivity, till Government roused it with the lash : that even then, from the respect and attachment which men are always inclined to show towards government, there still remained a large body of loyal Catholics ; that these only decreased in number from the rapid increase of persecution ; and that, after all, the effects which the resentment of the Roman Catholics had in creating rebellions had been very much exaggerated.

In support of these two conclusions, Mr. Parnell takes a survey of the history of Ireland, from the conquest under Henry to the rebellion under Charles I., passing very rapidly over the period which preceded the Reformation, and dwelling principally upon the various rebellions which broke out in Ireland between the Reformation and the grand rebellion in the reign of Charles I. The celebrated conquest of Ireland by Henry II. extended only to a very few counties in Leinster ; nine-tenths of the whole kingdom were left. as he found them, under the dominion of their native princes. The influence of example was as strong in this as in most other instances ; and great numbers of the English settlers who came over under various adventures resigned their pretensions to superior civilisation, cast off their lower garments, and lapsed into the nudity and barbarism of the Irish. The limit which divided the possessions of the English settler from those of the native Irish was called *the pale :* and the

expressions of inhabitants *within the pale*, and *without
the pale*, were the terms by which the two nations
were distinguished. It is almost superfluous to state,
that the most bloody and pernicious warfare was carried
on upon the borders—sometimes for something, sometimes for nothing—most commonly for cows. The Irish,
over whom the sovereigns of England affected a sort
of nominal dominion, were entirely governed by their
own laws, and so very little connection had they with
the justice of the invading country, that it was as
lawful to kill an Irishman as it was to kill a badger cr
a fox. The instances are innumerable, where the
defendant has pleaded that the deceased was an Irishman, and that therefore defendant had a right to kill
him—and upon the proof of Hibernicism, acquittal
followed of course.

When the English army mustered in any great
strength, the Irish chieftains would do exterior
homage to the English Crown; and they very frequently, by this artifice, averted from their country
the miseries of invasion : but they remained completely unsubdued, till the rebellion which took place
in the reign of Queen Elizabeth, of which that politic
woman availed herself to the complete subjugation of
Ireland. In speaking of the Irish about the reign
of Elizabeth or James I., we must not draw our
comparisons from England, but from New Zealand;
they were not civilised men, but savages ; and if we
reason about their conduct, we must reason of them as
savages.

"After reading every account of Irish history,"

says Mr. Parnell, "one great perplexity appears to remain: How does it happen, that, from the first invasion of the English till the reign of James I., Ireland seems not to have made the smallest progress in civilisation or wealth?

"That it was divided into a number of small principalities, which waged constant war on each other—or that the appointment of the chieftains was elective—do not appear sufficient reasons, although these are the only ones assigned by those who have been at the trouble of considering the subject: neither are the confiscations of property quite sufficient to account for the effect. There have been great confiscations in other countries, and still they have flourished; the petty states of Greece were quite analogous to the chiefries, as they were called, in Ireland; and yet they seemed to flourish almost in proportion to their dissensions. Poland felt the bad effects of an elective monarchy more than any other country; and yet, in point of civilisation, it maintained a very respectable rank among the nations of Europe; but Ireland never, for an instant, made any progress in improvement, till the reign of James I.

"It is scarcely credible, that in a climate like that of Ireland, and at a period so far advanced in civilisation as the end of Elizabeth's reign, the greater part of the natives should go naked. Yet this is rendered certain by the testimony of an eye-witness, Fynes Moryson. 'In the remote parts,' he says, 'where the English laws and manners are unknown, the very chief of the Irish, as well men as women, go naked in the winter

time, only having their privy parts covered with a rag
of linen, and their bodies with a loose mantle. This I
speak of my own experience; yet remember that a
Bohemian baron coming out of Scotland to us by the
north parts of the wild Irish, told me in great earnestness, that he, coming to the house of O'Kane, a great lord
amongst them, was met at the door by sixteen women,
all naked, excepting their loose mantles, whereof eight or
ten were very fair ; with which strange sight his eyes
being dazzled, they led him into the house, and then
sitting down by the fire, with crossed legs, like tailors,
and so low as could not but offend chaste eyes, desired
him to sit down with them. Soon after, O'Kane, the
lord of the country, came in all naked, except a loose
mantle and shoes, which he put off as soon as he came
in ; and, entertaining the Baron after his best manner
in the Latin tongue, desired him to put off his apparel,
which he thought to be a burden to him, and to sit
naked.

" ' To conclude, men and women at night going to
sleep, lie thus naked in a round circle about the fire,
with their feet towards it. They fold their heads and
their upper parts in woollen mantles, first steeped in
water to keep them warm; for they say, that woollen
cloth, wetted, preserves heat (as linen, wetted, preserves cold), when the smoke of their bodies has
warmed the woollen cloth.'

" The cause of this extreme poverty, and of its long
continuance, we must conclude, arose from the peculiar
laws of property which were in force under the Irish
dynasties. These laws have been described by most

writers as similar to the Kentish custom of gavelkind; and, indeed, so little attention was paid to the subject, that were it not for the researches of Sir J. Davis, the knowledge of this singular usage would have been entirely lost.

"The Brehon law of property, he tells us, was similar to the custom (as the English lawyers term it) of hodge-podge. When any one of the sept died, his lands did not descend to his sons, but were divided among the whole sept: and, for this purpose, the chief of the sept made a new division of the whole lands belonging to the sept, and gave every one his part according to seniority. So that no man had a property which could descend to his children; and even during his own life his possession of any particular spot was quite uncertain, being liable to be constantly shuffled and changed by new partitions. The consequence of this was that there was not a house of brick or stone among the Irish down to the reign of Henry VII.; not even a garden or orchard, or well-fenced or improved field; neither village or town, or in any respect the least provision for posterity. This monstrous custom, so opposite to the natural feelings of mankind, was probably perpetuated by the policy of the chiefs. In the first place the power of partitioning being lodged in their hands, made them the most absolute of tyrants, being the dispensers of the property as well as of the liberty of their subjects. In the second place, it had the appearance of adding to the number of their savage armies; for where there was no improvement or tillage, war was pursued as an occupation.

" In the early history of Ireland, we find several
instances of chieftains discountenancing tillage ; and
so late as Elizabeth's reign, Moryson says, that ' Sir
Neal Garve restrained his people from ploughing, that
they might assist him to do any mischief.' "—(pp. 99
—102).

These quotations and observations will enable us to
state a few plain facts for the recollection of our
English readers :—1st, Ireland was never subdued till
the rebellion in the reign of Queen Elizabeth. 2nd,
For four hundred years before that period the two
nations had been almost constantly at war ; and in
consequence of this, a deep and irreconcilable hatred
existed between the people within and without the
pale.   3rd, The Irish, at the accession of Queen
Elizabeth, were unquestionably the most barbarous
people in Europe.   So much for what had happened
previous to the reign of Queen Elizabeth ; and let any
man, who has the most superficial knowledge of human
affairs, determine whether national hatred, proceeding
from such powerful causes, could possibly have been
kept under by the defeat of one single rebellion—
whether it would not have been easy to have foreseen,
at that period, that a proud, brave, half-savage people,
would cherish the memory of their wrongs for centuries to come, and break forth into arms at every
period when they were particularly exasperated by oppression, or invited by opportunity.   If the Protestant
religion had spread in Ireland as it did in England,
and if there had never been any difference of faith

between the two countries—can it be believed that the
Irish, ill-treated and infamously governed as they have
been, would never have made any efforts to shake off
the yoke of England ? Surely there are causes enough
to account for their impatience of that yoke, without
endeavouring to inflame the zeal of ignorant people
against the Catholic religion, and to make that mode
of faith responsible for all the butchery which the
Irish and English for these last two centuries have
exercised upon each other. Everybody, of course,
must admit, that if to the causes of hatred already
specified there be added the additional cause of religious distinction, this last will give greater force (and
what is of more consequence to observe, give a *name*)
to the whole aggregate motive. But what Mr. Parnell
contends for, and clearly and decisively proves, is that
many of those sanguinary scenes attributed to the
Catholic religion are to be partly imputed to causes
totally disconnected from religion ; that the unjust
invasion, and the tyrannical, infamous policy of the
English, are to take their full share of blame with the
sophisms and plots of Catholic priests. In the reign
of Henry VIII., Mr. Parnell shows that feudal
submission was readily paid to him by all the Irish
chiefs ; that the Reformation was received without
the slightest opposition ; and that the troubles which
took place at that period in Ireland are to be entirely
attributed to the ambition and injustice of Henry. In
the reign of Queen Mary there was no recrimination
upon the Protestants—a striking proof that the
bigotry of the Catholic religion had not at that period

risen to any great height in Ireland. The insurrections of the various Irish princes were as numerous
during this reign as they had been in the two preceding reigns—a circumstance rather difficult of explana-
tion, if, as is commonly believed, the Catholic religion
was at that period the main-spring of men's actions.

In the reign of Elizabeth, the Catholic in the pale
regularly fought against the Catholic out of the pale.
O'Sullivan, a bigoted Papist, reproaches them with
doing so. Speaking of the reign of James I., he
says, "And now the eyes even of the English Irish
(the Catholics of the pale) were opened; and they
cursed their former folly for helping the heretic."
The English Government were so sensible of the
loyalty of the Irish English Catholics that they entrusted them with the most confidential services. The
Earl of Kildare was the principal instrument in
waging war against the chieftains of Leix and Offal.
William O'Bourge, another Catholic, was created
Lord Castle Connel for his eminent services; and
MacGully Patrick, a priest, was the State spy. We
presume that this wise and *manly* conduct of Queen
Elizabeth was utterly unknown both to the Pastrycook
and the Secretary of State, who have published upon
the dangers of employing Catholics even against
foreign enemies; and in those publications have said a
great deal about the wisdom of our ancestors—the
usual topic whenever the folly of their descendants is
to be defended. To whatever other of our ancestors
they may allude, they may spare all compliments to
this illustrious Princess, who would certainly have

kept the worthy confectioner to the composition of tarts, and most probably furnished him with the productions of the Right Honourable Secretary as the means of conveying those juicy delicacies to a hungry and discerning public.

In the next two reigns, Mr. Parnell shows by what injudicious measures of the English Government the spirit of Catholic opposition was gradually formed; for that it did produce powerful effects at a subsequent period he does not deny; but contends only (as we have before stated) that these effects have been much overrated, and ascribed *solely* to the Catholic religion when other causes have at least had an equal agency in bringing them about. He concludes with some general remarks on the dreadful state of Ireland, and the contemptible folly and bigotry of the English—remarks full of truth, of good sense, and of political courage. How melancholy to reflect, that there would be still some chance of saving England from the general wreck of empires, but that it may not be saved, because one politician will lose two thousand a year by it, and another three thousand—a third a place in reversion, and a fourth a pension for his aunt! Alas! these are the powerful causes which have always settled the destiny of great kingdoms, and which may level Old England, with all its boasted freedom, and boasted wisdom, to the dust. Nor is it the least singular, among the political phenomena of the present day, that the sole consideration which seems to influence the unbigoted part of the English people, in this great question of Ireland, is a regard for the personal feelings

of the Monarch. Nothing is said or thought of
the enormous risk to which Ireland is exposed—
nothing of the gross injustice with which the Catholics
are treated—nothing of the lucrative apostasy of those
from whom they experience this treatment: but the
only concern by which we all seem to be agitated is,
that the King must not be vexed in his old age. We
have a great respect for the King; and wish him all
the happiness compatible with the happiness of his
people. But these are not times to pay foolish compliments to kings, or the sons of kings, or to anybody
else; this journal (the *Edinburgh Review*) has always
preserved its character for courage and honesty; and
it shall do so to the last. If the people of this country
are solely occupied in considering what is personally
agreeable to the King, without considering what is for
his permanent good, and for the safety of his dominions; if all public men, quitting the common vulgar
scramble for emolument, do not concur in conciliating
the people of Ireland; if the unfounded alarms, and
the comparatively trifling interests of the clergy, are to
supersede the great question of freedom or slavery, it
does appear to us quite impossible that so mean and so
foolish a people can escape that destruction which is
ready to burst upon them—a destruction so imminent
that it can only be averted by arming all in our
defence who would evidently be sharers in our ruin—
and by such a change of system as may save us from
the hazard of being ruined by the ignorance and
cowardice of any general, by the bigotry or the ambition of any minister, or by the well-meaning scruples

of any human being, let his dignity be what it may. These minor and domestic dangers we must endeavour firmly and temperately to avert as we best can ; but at all hazards we must keep out the destroyer from among us, or perish like wise and brave men in the attempt.

IRELAND AND ENGLAND.

1. *Whitelaw's History of the City of Dublin.* 4to. Cadell and Davies.
2. *Observations on the State of Ireland, principally directed to its Agriculture and Rural Population; in a Series of Letters written on a Tour through that Country.* In 2 vols. By J. C. CURWEN, Esq., M.P. London, 1818.
3. *Gamble's Views of Society in Ireland.*

THESE are all the late publications that treat of Irish interests in general, and none of them are of first-rate importance. Mr. Gamble's "Travels in Ireland" are of a very ordinary description, low scenes and low humour making up the principal part of the narrative. There are readers, however, whom it will amuse; and the reading market becomes more and more extensive, and embraces a greater variety of persons every day. Mr. Whitelaw's "History of Dublin" is a book of great accuracy and research, highly creditable to the industry, good sense, and benevolence of its author. Of the "Travels" of Mr. Christian Curwen we hardly know what to say. He is bold and honest in his politics, a great enemy to abuses, vapid in his levity and pleasantry, and infinitely too much inclined to declaim upon commonplace topics of morality and benevolence. But, with these drawbacks, the book is not ill-written, and may be advantageously read by those who are desirous of information upon the present state of Ireland.

So great and so long has been the misgovernment of that country, that we verily believe the empire would be much stronger if everything was open sea between England and the Atlantic, and if *skates and cod-fish* swam over the fair land of Ulster. Such jobbing, such profligacy, so much direct tyranny and oppression, such an abuse of God's gifts, such a profanation of God's name for the purposes of bigotry and party spirit, cannot be exceeded in the history of civilised Europe, and will long remain a monument of infamy and shame to England. But it will be more useful to suppress the indignation which the very name of Ireland inspires, and to consider impartially those causes which have marred this fair portion of the creation, and kept it wild and savage in the midst of improving Europe.

The great misfortune of Ireland is that the mass of the people have been given up for a century to a handful of Protestants, by whom they have been treated as *Helots*, and subjected to every species of persecution and disgrace. The sufferings of the Catholics have been so loudly chanted in the very streets, that it is almost needless to remind our readers that, during the reigns of George I. and George II., the Irish Roman Catholics were disabled from holding any civil or military office, from voting at elections, from admission into corporations, from practising law or physic. A younger brother, by turning Protestant, might deprive his elder brother of his birthright; by the same process he might force his father, under the name of a liberal provision, to yield up to him a part of his landed property; and, if an eldest son, he might, in the same way, reduce his father's fee-simple to a life-estate. A Papist was disabled from purchasing freehold lands, and even from holding long leases; and any person might take his Catholic neighbour's house by paying £5 for it. If the child of a Catholic father turned Protestant he was taken away from his father and put into the hands of a Protestant relation. No Papist could purchase a freehold or lease for more than thirty years, or inherit from an intestate Protestant, nor from an intestate Catholic, nor dwell in Limerick or Galway, nor hold an advowson, nor buy an annuity for life. £50 was given for discovering a Popish archbishop, £30 for a Popish clergyman, and 10s. for a schoolmaster. No one was allowed to be trustee for Catholics; no Catholic was allowed to take more than two apprentices; no Papist to be solicitor, sheriff, or to serve on Grand Juries. Horses of Papists might be seized for the militia, for which militia Papists were to pay double, and to find Protestant substitutes. Papists were prohibited from being present at vestries, or from being high or petty constables: and, when resident in towns, they were compelled to find Protestant watchmen. Barristers and solicitors marrying Catholics were exposed to the penalties of Catholics. Persons plundered by privateers during a war with any Popish prince were reimbursed by a levy on the Catholic inhabitants where they lived. All Popish priests celebrating marriages contrary to 12 Geo. I., cap 3, were to be *hanged!*

The greater part of these incapacities are removed, though many of a very serious and oppressive nature still remain. But the grand misfortune is that the spirit which these oppressive laws engendered remains. The Protestant still looks upon the Catholic as a degraded being. The Catholic does not yet consider himself upon an equality with his former tyrant and taskmaster. That religious hatred which required all the prohibiting vigilance of the law for its restraint has found in the law its strongest support; and the spirit which the law first exasperated and embittered continues to act long after the original *stimulus* is withdrawn. The law which prevented Catholics from serving on Grand Juries is repealed; but Catholics are not called upon Grand Juries in the proportion in which they are entitled by their rank and fortune. The Duke of Bedford did all he could to give them the benefit of those laws which are already passed in their favour. But power is seldom entrusted in this country to one of the Duke of Bedford's liberality; and everything has fallen back in the hands of his successors into the ancient division of the privileged and degraded castes. We do not mean to cast any reflection upon the present Secretary for Ireland, whom we believe to be upon this subject a very liberal politician, and on all subjects an honourable and excellent man. The Government under which he serves allows him to indulge in a little harmless liberality; but it is perfectly understood that nothing is intended to be done for the Catholics; that no loaves and fishes will be lost by indulgence in Protestant insolence and tyranny; and, therefore, among the generality of Irish Protestants, insolence, tyranny, and exclusion continue to operate. However eligible the Catholic may be, he is not elected; whatever barriers may be thrown down, he does not advance a step. He was first kept out by law; he is now kept out by opinion and habit. They have been so long in chains that nobody believes they are capable of using their hands and feet.

It is not, however, the only or the worst misfortune of the Catholics that the relaxations of the law are hitherto of little benefit to them; the law is not yet sufficiently relaxed. A Catholic, as everybody knows, cannot be made sheriff; cannot be in parliament; cannot be a director of the Irish Bank; cannot fill the great departments of the law, the army, and the navy; is cut off from all the high objects of human ambition, and treated as a marked and degraded person.

The common admission now is that the Catholics are to the Protestants in Ireland as about four to one, of which Protestants not more than *one half* belong to the Church of Ireland. This, then, is one of the most striking features in the state of Ireland. That the great mass of the population is completely subjugated and overawed by a handful of comparatively recent settlers, in whom all the power and patronage of the country is vested, who have been reluctantly compelled to desist from still greater abuses of authority, and who look with trembling apprehension to the increasing liberality of the parliament and the country towards these unfortunate persons whom they have always looked upon as their property and their prey.

Whatever evils may result from these proportions between the oppressor and oppressed—to whatever dangers a country so situated may be considered to be exposed, these evils and dangers are rapidly increasing in Ireland. The proportion of Catholics to Protestants is infinitely greater now than it was thirty years' ago, and is becoming more and more favourable to the former. By a return made to the Irish House of Lords in 1732 the proportion of Catholics to Protestants was not two to one. It is now (as we have already observed) four to one; and the causes which have thus altered the proportions in favour of the Catholics are sufficiently obvious to any one acquainted with the state of Ireland. The Roman Catholic priest resides; his income entirely depends upon the number of his flock; and he must exert himself or he starves. There is some chance of success, therefore, in *his* efforts to convert; but the Protestant clergyman, if he were equally eager, has little or no probability of persuading so much larger a proportion of the population to come over to his Church. The Catholic clergyman belongs to a religion that has always been more desirous of gaining proselytes than the Protestant Church; and he is animated by a sense of injury and a desire of revenge. Another reason for the disproportionate increase of Catholics is that the Catholics will marry upon means which the Protestant considers as insufficient for marriage. A few potatoes and a shed of turf are all that Luther has left for the Romanist;

and, when the latter gets these, he instantly begins
upon the great Irish manufacture of children. But a
Protestant belongs to the sect that eats the fine flour
and leaves the bran to others; he must have comforts,
and he does not marry till he gets them. He would
be ashamed if he were seen living as a Catholic lives.
This is the principal reason why the Protestants who
remain attached to their Church do not increase so fast
as the Catholics. But in common minds, daily scenes,
the example of the majority, the power of imitation,
decide their habits, religious as well as civil. A
Protestant labourer who works among Catholics soon
learns to think and act and talk as they do; he is not
proof against the eternal panegyric which he hears of
Father O'Leary. His Protestantism is rubbed away,
and he goes at last, after some little resistance, to the
chapel where he sees everybody else going.

These eight Catholics not only hate the ninth man,
the Protestant of the Establishment, for the unjust
privileges he enjoys—not only remember that the lands
of their father were given to his father—but they find
themselves forced to pay for the support of his religion.
In the wretched state of poverty in which the lower
orders of Irish are plunged, it is not without considerable effort that they can pay the few shillings necessary
for the support of their Catholic priest; and when this
is effected, a tenth of the potatoes in the garden are to
be set out for the support of a persuasion, the introduction of which into Ireland they consider as the
great cause of their political inferiority, and all their
manifold wretchedness. In England a labourer can

procure constant employment, or he can, at the worst, obtain relief from his parish. Whether tithe operates as a tax upon him, is known only to the political economist: if he does pay it, he does not know that he pays it, and the burden of supporting the Clergy is at least kept out of his view. But in Ireland, the only method in which a poor man lives is by taking a small portion of land in which he can grow potatoes: seven or eight months out of twelve, in many parts of Ireland, there is no constant employment of the poor; and the potato farm is all that shelters them from absolute famine. If the Pope were to come in person, seize upon every tenth potato, the poor peasant would scarcely endure it. With what patience, then, can he see it tossed into the cart of the heretic rector, who has a church without a congregation, and a revenue without duties?

We do not say whether these things are right or wrong, whether they want a remedy at all, or what remedy they want; but we paint them in those colours in which they appear to the eye of poverty and ignorance, without saying whether those colours are false or true. Nor is the case at all comparable to that of Dissenters paying tithe in England; which case is precisely the reverse of what happens in Ireland, for it is the contribution of a very small minority to the religion of a very large majority; and the numbers on either side make all the difference in the argument. To exasperate the poor Catholic still more, the rich graziers of the parish, or the squire in his parish, pay no tithe at all for their grass land. Agistment tithe is abolished in Ireland, and the burthen of supporting two Churches seems to devolve upon the poorer Catholics, struggling with plough and spade in small scraps of dearly-rented land. Tithes seem to be collected in a more harsh manner than they are collected in England. The minute sub-divisions of land in Ireland—the little connection which the Protestant clergyman commonly has with the Catholic population of his parish—have made the introduction of tithe proctors very general, sometimes as the agent of the clergyman, sometimes as the lessee or middle-man between the clergyman and the cultivator of the land, but, in either case, practised, dexterous estimators of tithe. The English clergymen in general are far from exacting the whole of what is due to them, but sacrifice a little to the love of popularity or to the dread of odium. A system of tithe-proctors established all over England (as it is in Ireland), would produce general disgust and alienation from the Established Church.

"During the administration of Lord Halifax," says Mr. Hardy, in quoting the opinion of Lord Charlemont upon tithes paid by Catholics, "Ireland was dangerously disturbed in its southern and northern regions. In the south principally, in the counties of Kilkenny, Limerick, Cork, and Tipperary, the White Boys now made their first appearance; those White Boys who have ever since occasionally disturbed the public tranquillity, without any rational method having been as yet pursued to eradicate this disgraceful evil. When we consider that the very same district has been for

the long space of seven-and-twenty years liable to frequent returns of the same disorder into which it has
continually relapsed, in spite of all the violent remedies
from time to time administered by our political quacks,
we cannot doubt but that some real, peculiar, and
topical cause must exist, and yet neither the removal,
nor even the investigation of this cause, has ever once
been seriously attempted. Laws of the most sanguinary and unconstitutional nature have been enacted;
the country has been disgraced and exasperated by
frequent and bloody executions; and the gibbet, that
perpetual resource of weak and cruel legislators, has
groaned under the multitude of starving criminals;
yet, while the cause is suffered to exist, the effects will
ever follow. The amputation of limbs will never
eradicate a prurient humour, which must be sought in
its source and there remedied."

"I wish," continues Mr. Wakefield, "for the sake
of humanity and for the honour of the Irish character,
that the gentlemen of that country would take this
matter into their serious consideration. Let them only
for a moment place themselves in the situation of the
half-famished cotter, surrounded by a wretched family
clamorous for food, and judge what his feelings must
be when he sees the tenth part of the produce of his
potato garden exposed at harvest time to public *cant*,
or if he have given a promissory note for the payment
of a certain sum of money to compensate for such
tithe when it becomes due, to hear the heart-rending
cries of his offspring clinging round him, and
lamenting for the milk of which they are deprived by

the cows being driven to the pound to be sold to discharge the debt. Such accounts are not the creations
of fancy; the facts do exist, and are but too common
in Ireland. Were one of them transferred to canvas by
the hand of genius, and exhibited to English humanity,
that heart must be callous indeed that could refuse its
sympathy. I have seen the cow, the favourite cow,
driven away, accompanied by the sighs, the tears, and
the imprecations of a whole family, who were paddling
after, through wet and dirt, to take their last affectionate farewell of this their only friend and bene-
factor at the pound gate. I have heard with emotions
which I can scarcely describe, deep curses repeated
from village to village as the cavalcade proceeded. I
have witnessed the group pass the domain walls of the
opulent grazier, whose numerous herds were cropping
the most luxuriant pastures, while he was secure from
any demand for the tithe of their food, looking on with
the most unfeeling indifference."—*Ibid.*, p. 436.

In Munster, where tithe of potatoes is exacted,
risings against the system have constantly occurred
during the last forty years. In Ulster, where no such
tithe is required, these insurrections are unknown.
The double Church which Ireland supports, and that
painful visible contribution towards it which the poor
Irishman is compelled to make from his miserable
pittance, is one great cause of those never-ending insurrections, burnings, murders, and robberies, which
have laid waste that ill-fated country for so many
years. The unfortunate consequence of the civil dis-

abilities, and the Church payments under which the
Catholics labour, is a rooted antipathy to this country.
They hate the English Government from historical recollection, actual suffering, and disappointed hope, and
till they are better treated they will continue to hate
it. At this moment, in a period of the most profound
peace, there are twenty-five thousand of the best dis-
ciplined and best appointed troops in the world in
Ireland, with bayonets fixed, presented arms, and in
the attitude of present war: nor is there a man too
much—nor would Ireland be tenable without them.
When it was necessary last year (or thought necessary)
to put down the children of reform, we were forced to
make a new levy of troops in this country; not a man
could be spared from Ireland. The moment they had
embarked, Peep-of-Day Boys, Heart-of-Oak Boys,
Twelve-o'-clock Boys, Heart-of-Flint Boys, and all
the bloody boyhood of the Bog of Allen, would have
proceeded to the ancient work of riot, rapine, and disaffection. Ireland, in short, till her wrongs are re-
dressed and a more liberal policy is adopted towards
her, will always be a cause of anxiety and suspicion to
this country, and in some moment of our weakness and
depression, will forcibly extort what she would now
receive with gratitude and exultation.

Ireland is situated close to another island of greater
size, speaking the same language, very superior in
civilisation, and the seat of government. The consequence of this is the emigration of the richest and
most powerful part of the community—a vast drain
of wealth—and the absence of all that wholesome

influence which the representatives of ancient families, residing upon their estates, produce upon their tenantry and dependents. Can any man imagine that the scenes which have been acted in Ireland, within these last twenty years, would have taken place, if such vast proprietors as the Duke of Devonshire, the Marquis of Hertford, the Marquis of Lansdowne, Earl Fitzwilliam, and many other men of equal wealth, had been in the constant habit of residing upon their Irish as they are upon their English estates? Is it of no consequence to the order and the civilisation of a large district, whether the great mansion is inhabited by an insignificant, perhaps a mischievous attorney, in the shape of agent, or whether the first and greatest men of the United Kingdoms, after the business of Parliament is over, come with their friends and families, to exercise hospitality, to spend large revenues, to diffuse information, and to improve manners? This evil is a very serious one to Ireland; and, as far as we see, incurable. For if the present large estates were, by the dilapidation of families, to be broken to pieces and sold, others equally great would, in the free circulation of property, speedily accumulate; and the moment any possessor arrived at a certain pitch of fortune, he would probably choose to reside in the better country—near the Parliament, or the Court.

This absence of great proprietors in Ireland necessarily brings with it, or if not necessarily, has actually brought with it, the employment of the middlemen, which forms one other standing and regular Irish grievance. We are well aware of all that can be said

in defence of middlemen; that they stand between the
little farmer and the great proprietor as the shopkeeper
does between the manufacturer and consumer; and,
in fact, by their intervention, save time, and therefore
expense. This may be true enough in the abstract;
but the particular nature of land must be attended to.
The object of the man who makes cloth is to sell his
cloth at the present market, for as high a price as he
can obtain. If that price is too high, it soon falls;
but no injury is done to his machinery by the superior
price he has enjoyed for a season—he is just as able
to produce cloth with it, as if the profits he enjoyed
had always been equally moderate; he has no fear,
therefore, of the middleman, or of any species of moral
machinery which may help to obtain for him the
greatest present prices. The same would be the
feeling of any one who let out a steam-engine, or any
other machine, for the purposes of manufacture; he
would naturally take the highest price he could get;
for he might either let his machine for a price propor-
tionate to the work it did, or the repairs, estimable
with the greatest precision, might be thrown upon the
tenant; in short, he could hardly ask any rent too high
for his machine which a responsible person would
give; dilapidation would be so visible, and so cal-
culable in such instances, that any secondary lease,
or subletting, would be rather an increase of security
than a source of alarm. Any evil from such a practice
would be improbable, measurable, and remediable. In
land, on the contrary, the object is not to get the
highest prices absolutely, but to get the highest prices

which will not injure the machine. One tenant may
offer and pay double the rent of another, and in a few
years leave the land in a state which will effectually
bar all future offers of tenancy. It is of no use to fill
a lease full of clauses and covenants; a tenant who
pays more than he ought to pay, or who pays even to
the last farthing which he ought to pay, will rob the
land, and injure the machine, in spite of all the attor-
neys in England. He will rob it even if he means to
remain upon it—driven on by present distress, and
anxious to put off the day of defalcation and arrear.
The damage is often difficult of detection—not easily
calculated, not easily to be proved; such for which
juries (themselves perhaps farmers) will not willingly
give sufficient compensation. And if this be true in
England, it is much more strikingly true in Ireland,
where it is extremely difficult to obtain verdicts for
breaches of covenant in leases.

The only method, then, of guarding the machine
from real injury, is by giving to the actual occupier such
advantage in his contract, that he is unwilling to give
it up—that he has a real interest in retaining it, and is
not driven by the distresses of the present moment to
destroy the future productiveness of the soil. Any
rent which the landlord accepts more than this, or any
system by which more rent than this is obtained, is to
borrow money upon the most usurious and profligate
interest—to increase the revenue of the present day by
the absolute ruin of the property. Such is the effect
produced by a middleman; he gives high prices that
he may obtain higher from the occupier; more is paid

by the actual occupier than is consistent with the safety and preservation of the machine; the land is run out, and, in the end, that maximum of rent we have described is not obtained; and not only is the property injured by such a system, but in Ireland the most shocking consequences ensue from it. There is little manufacture in Ireland; the price of labour is low, the demand for labour irregular. If a poor man be driven, by distress of rent, from his potato garden, he has no other resource—all is lost: he will do the impossible (as the French say) to retain it; subscribe any bond, and promise any rent. The middleman has no character to lose; and he knew, when he took up the occupation, that it was one with which pity had nothing to do. On he drives; and backward the poor peasant recedes, loses something at every step, till he comes to the very brink of despair; and then he recoils and murders his oppressor, and is a *White Boy* or a *Right Boy*;—the soldier shoots him, and the judge hangs him.

In the debate which took place in the Irish House of Commons, upon the Bill for preventing tumultuous risings and assemblies, on the 31st of January, 1787, the Attorney-General submittted to the House the following narrative of facts.

"The commencement," said he, "was in one or two parishes in the county of Kerry; and they proceeded thus. The people assembled in a Catholic chapel, and there took an oath to obey the laws of Captain Right, and to starve the clergy. They then proceeded to the

next parishes on the following Sunday, and there swore
the people in the same manner; with this addition,
that they (the people last sworn) should on the ensuing
Sunday proceed to the chapels of their next neighbouring parishes and swear the inhabitants of those
parishes in like manner. Proceeding in this manner,
they very soon went through the province of Munster.
The first object was the *reformation of tithes.* They
swore not to give more than a certain price per acre,
not to assist or allow them to be assisted in drawing
the tithe, and to permit *no proctor.* They next took
upon them to prevent the collection of parish cesses,
next to nominate parish clerks, and in some cases
curates, to say what church should or should not be
repaired, and in one case to threaten that they would
burn a *new* church if the *old* one were not given for a
mass-house. At last they proceeded to regulate the
price of lands, to raise the price of labour, and to
oppose the collection of the hearth-money and other
taxes. Bodies of 5,000 of them have been seen to
march through the country unarmed, and, if met by
any magistrate, *they never offered the smallest rudeness
or offence;* on the contrary, they had allowed persons
charged with crimes to be taken from amongst them by
the magistrate *alone,* unaided by any force.

 " The Attorney-General said he was well acquainted
with the province of Munster, and that it was impossible for human wretchedness to *exceed that of the
peasantry of that province.* The unhappy tenantry
were *ground to powder* by relentless landlords; that,
far from being able to give the clergy their just dues,

they had not food or raiment for themselves—the
landlord grasped the whole; and sorry was he to add
that, not satisfied with the present extortion, some
landlords had been so base as to instigate the insur-
gents to rob the clergy of their tithes, not in order to
alleviate the distresses of the tenantry, but that they
might add the clergy's share to the cruel rack-rents
they already paid. The poor people of Munster lived
in a *more abject state of poverty than human
nature could be supposed equal to bear.*"—" Grattan's
Speeches," vol. i., p. 292.

We are not, of course, in such a discussion to be
governed by names. A middleman might be tied up
by the strongest legal restriction, as to the price he was
to exact from the under-tenants, and then he would be
no more pernicious to the estate than a steward. A
steward might be protected in exactions as severe as
the most rapacious middleman; and then, of course, it
would be the same thing under another name. The
practice to which we object is the too common method
in Ireland of extorting the last farthing which the
tenant is willing to give for land rather than quit it:
and the machinery by which such practice is carried
into effect is that of the middleman. It is not only
that it ruins the land; it ruins the people also. They
are made so poor—brought so near the ground—that
they can sink no lower; and burst out at last into all
the acts of desperation and revenge for which Ireland
is so notorious. Men who have money in their pockets,
and find that they are improving in their circumstances,

don't do these things. Opulence, or the hope of
opulence or comfort, is the parent of decency, order,
and submission to the laws. A landlord in Ireland
understands the luxury of carriages and horses, but
has no relish for the greater luxury of surrounding
himself with a moral and grateful tenantry. The
absent proprietor looks only to revenue, and cares
nothing for the disorder and degradation of a country
which he never means to visit. There are very honourable exceptions to this charge : but there are too many
living instances that it is just. The rapacity of the
Irish landlord induces him to allow of the extreme
division of his lands. When the daughter marries, a
little portion of the little farm is broken off—another
corner for Patrick, and another for Dermot—till the
land is broken into sections, upon one of which an
English cow could not stand. Twenty mansions of
misery are thus reared instead of one. A louder cry
of oppression is lifted up to heaven, and fresh enemies
to the English name and power are multiplied on the
earth. The Irish gentleman, too, extremely desirous
of political influence, multiplying freeholds, and split-
ting votes ; and this propensity tends of course to increase the miserable redundance of living beings,
under which Ireland is groaning. Among the manifold wretchedness to which the poor Irish tenant is
liable, we must not pass over the practice of driving
for rent. A lets land to B, who lets it to C, who lets
it again to D. D pays C his rent, and C pays B. But
if B fails to pay A, the cattle of B, C, D are all driven
to the pound, and after the interval of a few days sold

by auction. A general driving of this kind very frequently leads to a bloody insurrection. It may be
ranked among the classical grievances of Ireland.

Potatoes enter for a great deal into the present
condition of Ireland. They are much cheaper than
wheat; and it is so easy to rear a family upon them,
that there is no check to population from the difficulty
of procuring food. The population therefore goes on
with a rapidity approaching almost to that of new countries, and in a much greater ratio than the improving
agriculture and manufacturers of the country can find
employment for it. All degrees of all nations begin with
living in pig-styes. The king or the priest first gets
out of them; then the noble, then the pauper, in proportion as each class becomes more and more opulent.
Better tastes arise from better circumstances; and
the luxury of ✷one period is the wretchedness and
poverty of another. English peasants, in the time of
Henry VII., were lodged as badly as Irish peasants
now are; but the population was limited by the
difficulty of procuring a corn subsistence. The improvements of this kingdom were more rapid; the
price of labour rose; and with it the luxury and
comfort of the peasant, who is now decently lodged
and clothed, and who would think himself in the last
stage of wretchedness if he had nothing but an iron
pot in a turf house, and plenty of potatoes in it. The
use of the potato was introduced into Ireland when the
wretched accommodation of her own peasantry bore
some proportion to the state of those accommodations
all over Europe. But they have increased their popula-

tion so fast, and, in conjunction with the oppressive government of Ireland retarding improvement, have kept the price of labour so low, that the Irish poor have never been able to emerge from their mud cabins, or to acquire any taste for cleanliness and decency of appearance. Mr. Curwen has the following description of Irish cottages :—

"These mansions of miserable existence, for so they may truly be described, conformably to our general estimation of those indispensable comforts requisite to constitute the happiness of rational beings, are most commonly composed of two rooms on the ground floor, a most appropriate term, for they are literally on the earth, the surface of which is not unfrequently reduced a foot or more to save the expense of so much outward walling. The one is a refectory, the other the dormitory. The furniture of the former, if the owner ranks in the upper part of the scale of scantiness, will consist of a kitchen dresser, well provided and highly decorated with crockery—not less apparently the pride of the husband than the result of female vanity in the wife : which, with a table, a chest, a few stools, and an iron pot, complete the catalogue of conveniences generally found as belonging to the cabin : while a spinning-wheel, furnished by the Linen Board, and a loom, ornament vacant spaces that otherwise would remain unfurnished. In fitting up the latter, which cannot on any occasion or by any display add a feather to the weight or importance expected to be excited by the appearance of the former, the inventory is limited to

one, and sometimes two beds, serving for the repose of
the whole family! However downy these may be to
limbs impatient for rest, their coverings appear to be
very slight, and the whole of the apartment created
reflections of a very painful nature. Under such privations, with a wet mud floor and a roof in tatters, how
idle.the search for comforts!"—*Curwen*, i., pp. 112,
113.

To this extract we shall add one more on the same
subject.

"The gigantic figure, bareheaded before me, had a
beard that would not have disgraced an ancient Israel-
ite—he was without shoes or stockings—and almost a
sans-culotte—with a coat, or rather a jacket, that appeared as if the first blast of wind would tear it to
tatters. Though his garb was thus tattered, he had a
manly commanding countenance. I asked permission
to see the inside of his cabin, to which I received his
most courteous assent. On stooping to enter at the
door I was stopped, and found that permission from
another was necessary before I could be admitted. A
pig, which was fastened to a stake driven into the floor,
with length of rope sufficient to permit him the enjoyment of sun and air, demanded some courtesy, which I
showed him, and was suffered to enter. The wife was
engaged in boiling thread, and by her side, near the fire,
a lovely infant was sleeping, without any covering, on
a bare board. Whether the fire gave additional glow to
the countenance of the babe, or that Nature impressed
on its unconscious cheek a blush that the lot of man

should be exposed to such privations, I will not decide;
but if the cause be referable to the latter, it was in
perfect unison with my own feelings. Two or three
other children crowded round the mother: on their
rosy countenances health seemed established in spite
of filth and ragged garments. The dress of the poor
woman was barely sufficient to satisfy decency. Her
countenance bore the expression of a set melancholy,
tinctured with an appearance of ill health. The hovel,
which did not exceed twelve or fifteen feet in length
and ten in breadth, was half obscured by smoke—
chimney or window I saw none; the door served the
various purposes of an inlet to light and the outlet to
smoke. The furniture consisted of two stools, an iron
pot, and a spinning-wheel, while a sack stuffed with
straw, and a single blanket laid on planks, served as a
bed for the repose of the whole family. Need I attempt
to describe my sensations? The statement alone cannot fail of conveying to a mind like yours an adequate
idea of them—I could not long remain a witness to
this acme of human misery. As I left the deplorable
habitation the mistress followed me to repeat her thanks
for the trifle I had bestowed. This gave me an opportunity of observing her person more particularly. She
was a tall figure, her countenance composed of interesting features, and with every appearance of having
once been handsome.

"Unwilling to quit the village without first satisfy-
ing myself whether what I had seen was a solitary
instance or a sample of its general state, or whether the
extremity of poverty I had just beheld had arisen from

peculiar improvidence and want of management in one wretched family, I went into an adjoining habitation, where I found a poor old woman of eighty, whose miserable existence was painfully continued by the maintenance of her granddaughter. Their condition, if possible, was more deplorable."—*Curwen*, i., pp. 181 —183.

This wretchedness, of which all strangers who visit Ireland are so sensible, proceeds certainly in great measure from their accidental use of a food so cheap, that it encourages population to an extraordinary degree, lowers the price of labour, and leaves the multitudes which it calls into existence almost destitute of everything but food. Many more live in consequence of the introduction of potatoes; but all live in greater wretchedness. In the progress of population, the potato must of course become at last as difficult to be procured as any other food; and then let the political economist calculate what the immensity and wretchedness of a people must be, where the further progress of population is checked by the difficulty of procuring potatoes.

The consequence of the long mismanagement and oppression of Ireland, and of the singular circumstances in which it is placed, is, that it is a semi-barbarous country — more shame to those who have thus ill-treated a fine country and a fine people; but it is part of the present case of Ireland. The barbarism of Ireland is evinced by the frequency and ferocity of duels —the hereditary clannish feuds of the common people

and the fights to which they give birth—the atrocious
cruelties practised in the insurrections of the common
people—and their proneness to insurrection. The lower
Irish live in a state of greater wretchedness than any
other people in Europe inhabiting so fine a soil and
climate. It is difficult, often impossible, to execute the
processes of law. In cases where gentlemen are concerned, it is often not even attempted. The conduct of
under-sheriffs is often very corrupt. We are afraid
the magistracy of Ireland is very inferior to that of this
country; the spirit of jobbing and bribery is very
widely diffused, and upon occasions when the utmost
purity prevails in the sister kingdom. Military force
is necessary all over the country, and often for the most
common and just operations of Government. The behaviour of the higher to the lower orders is much less
gentle and decent than in England. Blows from superiors to inferiors are more frequent, and the punish-
ment for such aggression more doubtful. The word
gentleman seems, in Ireland, to put an end to most processes at law. Arrest a gentleman!!!—take out a
warrant against a gentleman—are modes of operation
not very common in the administration of Irish justice.
If a man strike the meanest peasant in England, he is
either knocked down in his turn, or immediately taken
before a magistrate. It is impossible to live in Ireland
without perceiving the various points in which it is
inferior in civilisation. Want of unity in feeling and
interest among the people—irritability, violence, and
revenge—want of comfort and cleanliness in the lower
orders—habitual disobedience to the law—want of

confidence in magistrates—corruption, venality, the perpetual necessity of recurring to military force—all carry back the observer to that remote and early condition of mankind, which an Englishman can learn only in the pages of the antiquary or the historian. We do not draw this picture for censure but for truth. We admire the Irish—feel the most sincere pity for the state of Ireland—and think the conduct of the English to that country to have been a system of atrocious cruelty and contemptible meanness. With such a climate, such a soil, and such a people, the inferiority of Ireland to the rest of Europe is directly chargeable to the long wickedness of the English Government.

A direct consequence of the present uncivilised state of Ireland is, that very little English capital travels there. The man who deals in steam-engines, and warps and woofs, is naturally alarmed by Peep-of-Day Boys, and nocturnal Carders; his object is to buy and sell as quickly and quietly as he can, and he will naturally bear high taxes and rivalry in England, or emigrate to any part of the Continent, or to America, rather than plunge into the tumult of Irish politics and passions. There is nothing which Ireland wants more than large manufacturing towns to take off its superfluous population. But internal peace must come first, and then the arts of peace will follow. The foreign manufacturer will hardly think of embarking his capital where he cannot be sure that his existence is safe. Another check to the manufacturing greatness of Ireland is the scarcity, not of coal, but of good coal, cheaply raised—an article in which (in

spite of papers in the Irish Transactions) they are
lamentably inferior to the English.

Another consequence from some of the causes we
have stated is the extreme idleness of the Irish
labourer. There is nothing of the value of which the
Irish seem to have so little notion as that of time.
They scratch, pick, dawdle, stare, gape, and do anything but strive and wrestle with the task before
them. The most ludicrous of all human objects is an
Irishman ploughing. A gigantic figure—a seven-foot
machine for turning potatoes in human nature—wrapt
up in an immense great-coat, and urging on two
starved ponies, with dreadful imprecations and uplifted
shillala. The Irish crow discerns a coming perquisite,
and is not inattentive to the proceedings of the steeds.
The furrow which is to be the depository of the future
crop is not unlike, either in depth or regularity, to
those domestic furrows which the nails of the meek
and much-injured wife plough, in some family quarrel,
upon the cheeks of the deservedly punished husband.
The weeds seem to fall contentedly, knowing that they
have fulfilled their destiny, and left behind them, for
the resurrection of the ensuing spring, an abundant
and healthy progeny. The whole is a scene of idleness, laziness, and poverty, of which it is impossible,
in this active and enterprising country, to form the
most distant conception; but strongly indicative of
habits, whether secondary or original, which will long
present a powerful impediment to the improvement of
Ireland.

The Irish character contributes something to retard

the improvements of that country. The Irishman has many good qualities: he is brave, witty, generous, eloquent, hospitable, and open-hearted; but he is vain, ostentatious, extravagant, and fond of display, light in counsel, deficient in perseverance, without skill in private or public economy, an enjoyer; not an acquirer —one who despises the slow and patient virtues—who wants the superstructure without the foundation, the result without the previous operation, the oak without the acorn and the three hundred years of expectation. The Irish are irascible, prone to debt and to fight, and very impatient of the restraints of law. Such a people are not likely to keep their eyes steadily upon the main chance like the Scotch or the Dutch. England strove very hard at one period to compel the Scotch to pay a double Church, but Sawney took his pen and ink, and finding what a sum it amounted to became furious and drew his sword. God forbid the Irishman should do the same! The remedy now would be worse than the disease; but if the oppressions of England had been more steadily resisted a century ago, Ireland would not have been the scene of poverty, misery, and distress which it now is.

The Catholic religion, among other causes, contributes to the backwardness and barbarism of Ireland. Its debasing superstition, childish ceremonies, and the profound submission to the priesthood which it teaches, all tend to darken men's minds, to impede the progress of knowledge and inquiry, and to prevent Ireland from becoming as free, as powerful, and as rich as the sister kingdom. Though sincere friends to Catholic emancipation, we are no advocates for the Catholic religion. We should be very glad to see a general conversion to Protestantism among the Irish, but we do not think that violence, privations, and incapacities, are the proper methods of making proselytes.

Such, then, is ·Ireland at this period—a land more barbarous than the rest of Europe, because it has been worse treated and more cruelly oppressed. Many of the incapacities and privations to which the Catholics were exposed have been removed by law, but in such instances they are still incapacitated and deprived by custom. Many cruel and oppressive laws are still enforced against them. A tenth part of the population engrosses all the honours of the country; the other nine pay a tenth of the product of the earth for the support of a religion in which they do not believe. There is little capital in the country. The great and rich men are called by business, or allured by pleasure, into England; their estates are given up to factors, and the utmost farthing of rent extorted from the poor, who, if they give up the land, cannot get employment in manufactures, or regular employment in husbandry. The common people use a sort of food so very cheap that they can rear families who cannot procure employment, and who have little more of the comforts of life than food. The Irish are light-minded—want of employment has made them idle; they are irritable and brave, have a keen remembrance of the past wrongs they have suffered, and the present wrongs they are suffering from England. The consequence of all this is, eternal riot and insurrection, a whole army of soldiers in time of profound peace, and general rebellion whenever England is busy with her other enemies or off her guard ! And thus it will be, while the same causes continue to operate, for ages to come, and worse and worse as the rapidly increasing population of the Catholics becomes more and more numerous.

The remedies are time and justice, and that justice consists in repealing all laws which make any distinction between the two religions; in placing over the government of Ireland, not the stupid, amiable, and insignificant noblemen who have too often been sent there, but men who feel deeply the wrongs of Ireland, and who have an ardent wish to heal them; who will take care that Catholics, when eligible, shall be elected; who will share the patronage of Ireland proportionally among the two parties, and give to just and liberal laws the same vigour of execution which has hitherto been reserved only for decrees of tyranny, and the enactments of oppression. The injustice and hardship of supporting two Churches must be put out of sight, if it cannot or ought not to be cured. The political economist, the moralist, and the satirist, must combine to teach moderation and superintendence to the great Irish proprietors. Public talk and clamour may do something for the poor Irish, as it did for the slaves in the West Indies. Ireland will become more quiet under such treatment, and then more rich, more comfortable, and more civilised ; and the horrid spectacle of folly and tyranny, which it at present exhibits, may in time be removed from the eyes of Europe.

There are two eminent Irishmen now in the House
of Commons—Lord Castlereagh and Mr. Canning—
who will subscribe to the justness of every syllable we
have said upon this subject, and who have it in their
power, by making it the condition of their remaining
in office, to liberate their native country, and raise it to
its just rank among the nations of the earth.   Yet the
Court buys them over, year after year, by the pomp
and perquisites of office; and year after year they come
into the House of Commons, feeling deeply, and describing powerfully, the injuries of five millions of their
countrymen—and *continue* members of a government
that inflicts those evils, under the pitiful delusion that
it is not a Cabinet Question, as if the scratchings and
quarrellings of Kings and Queens could alone cement
politicians together in indissoluble unity, while the fate
and fortune of one-third of the empire might be com-
plimented away from one minister to another, without
the smallest breach in their Cabinet alliance.   Politicians, at least honest politicians, should be very flexible
and accommodating in little things, very rigid and inflexible in great things.   And is this *not* a great thing?
Who has painted it in finer and more commanding
eloquence than Mr. Canning?   Who has taken a more
sensible and statesmanlike view of our miserable and
cruel policy than Lord Castlereagh?   You would think,
to hear them, that the same planet could not contain
them and the oppressors of their country—perhaps
not the same solar system.   Yet for money, claret,
and patronage, they lend their countenance, assistance,
and friendship to the Ministers who are the stern

and inflexible enemies to the emancipation of Ireland!

Thank God that all is not profligacy and corruption in the history of that devoted people—and that the name of Irishman does not always carry with it the idea of the oppressor or the oppressed—the plunderer or the plundered—the tyrant or the slave! Great men hallow a whole people, and lift up all who live in their time. What Irishman does not feel proud that he has lived in the days of GRATTAN? who has not turned to him for comfort, from the false friends and open enemies of Ireland? who did not remember him in the days of its burnings and wastings and murders? No Government ever dismayed him—the world could not bribe him—he thought only of Ireland—lived for no other object—dedicated to her his beautiful fancy, his elegant wit, his manly courage, and all the splendour of his astonishing eloquence. He was so born and so gifted that poetry, forensic skill, elegant literature, and all the highest attainments of human genius were within his reach; but he thought the noblest occupation of a man was to make other men happy and free; and in that straight line he went on for fifty years, without one side-look, without one yielding thought, without one motive in his heart which he might not have laid open to the view of God and man. He is gone!—but there is not a single day of his honest life of which every good Irishman would not be more proud than of the whole political existence of his countrymen—the annual deserters and betrayers of their native land.

MOORE'S CAPTAIN ROCK.

Memoirs of Captain Rock, the celebrated Irish Chieftain; with some Account of his Ancestors. Written by Himself. Fourth Edition. 12mo. London, 1824.

THIS agreeable and witty book is generally supposed to have been written by Mr. Thomas Moore, a gentleman of small stature, but full of genius, and a steady friend of all that is honourable and just. He has here borrowed the name of a celebrated Irish leader, to typify that spirit of violence and insurrection which is necessarily generated by systematic oppression, and rudely avenges its crimes; and the picture he has drawn of its prevalence in that unhappy country is at once piteous and frightful. Its effect in exciting our horror and indignation is in the long run increased, we think— though at first it may seem counteracted—by the tone of levity, and even jocularity, under which he has chosen to veil the deep sarcasm and substantial terrors of his story. We smile at first, and are amused, and wonder, as we proceed, that the humorous narrative should produce conviction and pity—shame, abhorrence, and despair.

England seems to have treated Ireland much in the same way as Mrs. Brownrigg treated her apprentice— for which Mrs. Brownrigg is hanged in the first volume of the Newgate Calendar. Upon the whole, we think the apprentice is better off than the Irishman; as

Mrs. Brownrigg merely starves and beats her, without any attempt to prohibit her from going to any shop, or praying at any church her apprentice might select: and once or twice, if we remember rightly, Brownrigg appears to have felt some compassion. Not so Old England, who indulges rather in a steady baseness, uniform brutality, and unrelenting oppression.

Let us select from this entertaining little book a short history of dear Ireland, such as even some profligate idle member of the House of Commons, voting as his master bids him, may perchance throw his eye upon, and reflect for a moment upon the iniquity to which he lends his support.

For some centuries after the reign of Henry II., the Irish were killed like game, by persons qualified or unqualified. Whether dogs were used does not appear quite certain, though it is probable they were, spaniels as well as pointers; and that, after a regular point by Basto, well backed by Ponto and Cæsar, Mr. O'Donnel or Mr. O'Leary bolted from the thicket, and were bagged by the English sportsman. With Henry II. came in tithes, to which, in all probability, about one million of lives may have been sacrificed in Ireland. In the reign of Edward I. the Irish who were settled near the English requested that the benefit of the English laws might be extended to them; but the remonstrance of the barons with the hesitating king was in substance this: "You have made us a present of these wild gentlemen, and we particularly request that no measures may be adopted to check us in that full range of tyranny and oppression in which we consider the value of such

a gift to consist.   You might as well give us sheep, and
prevent us from shearing the wool, or roasting the
meat."   This reasoning prevailed, and the Irish were
kept to their barbarism, and the barons preserved their
live stock.

"Read 'Orange faction' (says Captain Rock) here and
you have the wisdom of our rulers, at the end of near
six centuries, *in statu quo.*   The grand periodic year of
the stoics, at the close of which everything was to begin
again, and the same events to be all reacted in the same
order, is, on a miniature scale, represented in the history
of the English Government in Ireland, every succeeding
century being but a new revolution of the same follies,
the same crimes, and the same turbulence that disgraced
the former.   But ' Vive l'ennemi ! ' say I : whoever
may suffer by such measures, Captain Rock, at least,
will prosper.

" And such was the result at the period of which I
am speaking.   The rejection of a petition, so humble
and so reasonable, was followed, as a matter of course,
by one of those daring rebellions into which the revenge
of an insulted people naturally breaks forth.   The
M'Cartys, the O'Briens, and the other Macs and O's,
who have been kept on the alert by similar causes ever
since, flew to arms under the command of a chieftain
of my family ; and, as the proffered *handle* of the sword
had been rejected, made their inexorable masters at
least feel its *edge.*"—(pp. 23—25.)

Fifty years afterwards the same request was renewed
and refused.   Up again rose Mac and O, a *just and*

necessary war ensued; and after the usual murders, the usual chains were replaced upon the Irishry. All Irishmen were excluded from every species of office. It was high treason to marry with the Irish blood, and highly penal to receive the Irish into religious houses. War was waged also against their Thomas Moores, Samuel Rogerses, and Walter Scotts, who went about the country harping and singing against English oppression. No such turbulent guests were to be received. The plan of making them poets-laureate, or converting them to loyalty by pensions of £100 per annum, had not then been thought of. They debarred the Irish even from the pleasure of running away, and fixed them to the soil like negroes.

"I have thus selected," says the historian of Rock, "cursorily and at random, a few features of the reigns preceding the Reformation, in order to show what good use was made of those three or four hundred years in attaching the Irish people to their English governors; and by what a gentle course of alternatives they were prepared for the inoculation of a new religion, which was now about to be attempted upon them by the same skilful and friendly hands.

"Henry VII. appears to have been the first monarch to whom it occurred, that matters were not managed exactly as they ought in this part of his dominions; and we find him—with a simplicity which is still fresh and youthful among our rulers—expressing his *surprise* that 'his subjects of this land should be so prone to faction and rebellion, and that so little ad-

vantage had been hitherto derived from the acquisitions
of his predecessor, notwithstanding the fruitfulness
and natural advantages of Ireland. Surprising, indeed,
that a policy, such as we have been describing, should
not have converted the whole country into a perfect
Atlantis of happiness—should not have made it like
the imaginary island of Sir Thomas More, where ' *tota
insula velut una familia est !*'—most stubborn, truly,
and ungrateful, must that people be, upon whom, up to
the very hour in which I write, such a long and un-
varying course of penal laws, confiscations, and Insurrection Acts has been tried, without making them in
the least degree in love with their rulers.

" Heloise tells her tutor, Abelard, that the correction
which he inflicted upon her only served to increase the
ardour of her affection for him ; but bayonets and hemp
are no such '*amoris stimuli.*' One more character-
istic anecdote of those times and I have done. At the
battle of Knocktow, in the reign of Henry VII., when
that remarkable man, the Earl of Kildare, assisted by
the great O'Neal and other Irish chiefs, gained a victory
over Clanricard of Connaught, most important to the
English Government, Lord Gormanstown, after the
battle, in the first insolence of success, said, turning to
the Earl of Kildare, ' We have now slaughtered our
enemies, but, to complete the good deed, we must proceed yet further, and—cut the throats of those Irish of
our own party ! ' Who can wonder that the Rock
family were active in those times ? "—(pp. 33, 35.)

Henry VIII. persisted in all these outrages, and

aggravated them by insulting the prejudices of the people. England is almost the only country in the world (even at present) where there is not some favourite religious sport, where absurd lies, little bits of cloth, feathers, rusty nails, splinters, and other invaluable relics, are treasured up, and in defence of which the whole population are willing to turn out and perish as one man. Such was the shrine of St. Kieran, the whole treasures of which the satellites of that corpulent tyrant turned out into the street, pillaged the sacred church of Clonmacnoise, scattered the holy nonsense of the priests to the winds, and burnt the real and venerable crosier of St. Patrick, fresh from the silversmith's shop, and formed of the most costly materials. Modern princes change the uniform of regiments; Henry changed the religion of kingdoms, and was determined that the belief of the Irish should undergo a radical and Protestant conversion. With what success this attempt was made, the present state of Ireland is sufficient evidence.

"Be not dismayed," said Elizabeth, on hearing that O'Neal meditated some designs against her government; "tell my friends, if he arise, it will turn to their advantage—*there will be estates for those who want.*" Soon after this prophetic speech, Munster was destroyed by famine and the sword, and near 600,000 acres forfeited to the crown, and distributed among Englishmen. Sir Walter Raleigh (the virtuous and good) butchered the garrison of Limerick in cold blood, after Lord Deputy Gray had selected 700 to be hanged. There were, during the reign of Elizabeth, three invasions of

Ireland by the Spaniards, produced principally by the absurd measures of this princess for the reformation of its religion. The Catholic clergy, in consequence of these measures, abandoned their cures, the churches fell to ruin, and the people were left without any means of instruction. Add to these circumstances the murder of M'Mahon, the imprisonment of O'Toole and O'Dogherty, and the kidnapping of O'Donnel—all truly Anglo-Hibernian proceedings. The execution of the laws was rendered detestable and intolerable by the queen's officers of justice. The spirit raised by these transactions, besides innumerable smaller insurrections, gave rise to the great wars of Desmond and Hugh O'Neal; which, after they had worn out the ablest generals, discomfited the choicest troops, exhausted the treasure, and embarrassed the operations of Elizabeth, were terminated by the destruction of these two ancient families, and by the confiscation of more than half the territorial surface of the island. The last two years of O'Neal's wars cost Elizabeth £140,000 per annum, though the whole revenue of England at that period fell considerably short of £500,000. Essex, after the destruction of Norris, led into Ireland an army of above 20,000 men, which was totally baffled and destroyed by Tyrone, within two years of their landing. Such was the importance of Irish rebellions two centuries before the time in which we live. Sir G. Carew attempted to assassinate the Lugan Earl—Mountjoy compelled the Irish rebels to massacre each other. In the course of a few months 3,000 men were starved to death in Tyrone. Sir Arthur Chichester, Sir Richard Manson, and other commanders, saw three children feeding on the flesh of their dead mother. Such were the golden days of good Queen Bess!

By the rebellions of Dogherty, in the reign of James I., six northern counties were confiscated, amounting to 500,000 acres. In the same manner, 64,000 acres were confiscated in Athlone. The whole of his confiscations amount to nearly a million acres; and if Leland means plantation acres, they constitute a twelfth of the whole kingdom according to Newenham, and a tenth according to Sir W. Petty. The most shocking and scandalous action in the reign of James, was his attack upon the whole property of the province of Connaught, which he would have effected, if he had not been bought off by a sum greater than he hoped to gain by his iniquity, besides the luxury of confiscation. The Irish, during the reign of James I., suffered under the *double* evils of a licentious soldiery and a religious persecution.

Charles I. took a bribe of £120,000 from his Irish subjects, to grant them what in those days were called *Graces*, but in these days would be denominated the Elements of Justice. The money was paid, but the graces were never granted. One of these graces was curious enough : " That the clergy were not to be permitted to keep henceforward any private prisons of their own, but delinquents were to be committed to the public jails." The idea of a rector, with his own private jail full of Dissenters, is the most ludicrous piece of tyranny we ever heard of. The troops in the beginning of Charles's reign were supported by the weekly fines levied upon the Catholics for non-attendance upon established worship. The Archbishop of Dublin went himself at the head of a file of musketeers, to disperse a Catholic congregation in Dublin—which object he effected after a considerable skirmish with the priests. "The favourite object" (says Dr. Leland, a Protestant clergyman, and dignitary of the Irish Church) "of the Irish Government and the English Parliament, was *the utter extermination* of all the Catholic inhabitants of Ireland." The great rebellion took place in this reign, and Ireland was one scene of blood and cruelty and confiscation.

Cromwell began his career in Ireland by massacring for five days the garrison of Drogheda, to whom quarter had been promised. Two millions and a half of acres were confiscated. Whole towns were put up in lots, and sold. The Catholics were banished from three-fourths of the kingdom, and confined to Connaught. After a certain day, every Catholic found out of Connaught was to be punished with death. Fleetwood complains peevishly "that the people *do not transport readily*," but adds, "*it is doubtless a work in which the Lord will appear.*" Ten thousand Irish were sent as recruits to the Spanish army.

"Such was *Cromwell's* way of settling the affairs of Ireland; and if a nation *is* to be ruined, this method is, perhaps, as good as any. It is, at least, more humane than the slow, lingering process of exclusion, disappointment, and degradation, by which their hearts are worn out under more specious forms of tyranny; and that talent of despatch which Molière attributes

to one of his physicians is no ordinary merit in a
practitioner like Cromwell:—"C'est un homme expé-
ditif, qui aime à depêcher ses malades; et quand on à
mourir, cela se fait avec lui le plus vite du monde."
A certain military Duke, who complains that Ireland
is but half conquered, would, no doubt, upon an
emergency, try his hand in the same line of practice,
and, like that 'stern hero' Mirmillo, in the Dispensary,

> " While others meanly take whole months to slay,
> Despatch the grateful patient in a day ! "

"Among other amiable enactments against the
Catholics at this period, the price of five pounds was
set on the head of a Romish priest, being exactly the
same sum offered by the same legislators for the head
of a wolf. The Athenians, we are told, encouraged
the destruction of wolves by a similar reward (five
drachms); but it does not appear that these heathens
bought up the heads of priests at the same rate, such
zeal in the cause of religion being reserved for times.
of Christianity and Protestantism."—(pp. 97—99.)

Nothing can show more strongly the light in which
the Irish were held by Cromwell than the correspondence with Henry Cromwell respecting the peopling
of Jamaica from Ireland. Secretary Thurloe sends to
Henry, the Lord Deputy in Ireland, to inform him
that "a stock of Irish girls and Irish young men are
wanting for the peopling of Jamaica." The answer of
Henry Cromwell is as follows:—"Concerning the
supply of young men, although we must use force in
taking them up, *yet it being so much for their own*

good, and likely to be of so great advantage to the
public, it is not the least doubted but that you may
have such a number of them as you may think fit to
make use of on this account.

"I shall not need repeat anything respecting the
girls, not doubting to answer your expectations to the
full *in that*; and I think it might be of like advantage
to your affairs there and ours here if you should think
fit to send 1,500 or 2,000 boys to the place above
mentioned. *We can well spare them*; and who knows
but that it may be the means of making them Englishmen—I mean, rather, Christians? As for the girls, I
suppose you will make provisions of clothes, and other
accommodations for them." Upon this, Thurloe in-
forms Henry Cromwell that the council have voted
4,000 *girls, and as many boys*, to go to Jamaica.

Every Catholic priest found in Ireland was hanged,
and five pounds paid to the informer.

"About the years 1652 and 1653," says Colonel
Lawrence, in his *Interests of Ireland*, "the plague and
famine had so swept away whole counties, that a man
might travel twenty or thirty miles and not see a
living creature, either man, or beast, or bird, they
being all dead, or had quitted those desolate places.
Our soldiers would tell stories of the places where they
saw smoke—it was so rare to see either smoke by day
or fire or candle by night." In this manner did the
Irish live and die under Cromwell, suffering by the
sword, famine, pestilence, and persecution, beholding
the confiscation of a kingdom and the banishment of a

race. "So that there perished," says Sir W. Petty. "in the year 1641, 650,000 human beings, whose blood somebody must atone for to God and the King!"

In the reign of Charles II., by the Act of Settlement, four millions and a half of acres were for ever taken from the Irish. "This country," says the Earl of Essex, Lord Lieutenant in 1675, "has been perpetually rent and torn since his Majesty's restoration. I can compare it to nothing better than the flinging the reward on the death of a deer among the pack of hounds. where every one pulls and tears where he can for himself." All wool grown in Ireland was, by Act of Parliament, compelled to be sold to England; and Irish cattle were excluded from England. The English, however, were pleased to accept 30,000 head of cattle, sent as a gift from Ireland to the sufferers in the great fire♦ and the first day of the Sessions, after this act of munificence, the Parliament passed fresh acts of exclusion against the productions of that country.

"Among the many anomalous situations in which the Irish have been placed, by those 'marriage vows, false as dicers' oaths,' which bind their country to England, the dilemma in which they found themselves at the Revolution was not the less perplexing or cruel. If they were loyal to the King *de jure,* they were hanged by the King *de facto ;* and if they escaped with life from the King *de facto,* it was but to be plundered and proscribed by the King *de jure* afterwards.

"' Hac *gener* atque *socer* coeunt mercede suorum.'—VIRGIL.

"' In a manner so summary, prompt, and high mettled,
Twixt father and son-in-law matters were settled.'

"In fact, most of the outlawries in Ireland were for treason committed the very day on which the Prince and Princess of Orange accepted the crown in the Banqueting-house; though the news of this event could not possibly have reached the other side of the Channel on the same day, and the Lord-Lieutenant of King James, with an army to enforce obedience, was at that time in actual possession of the government, so little was common sense consulted, or the mere decency of forms observed, by that rapacious spirit, which nothing less than the confiscation of the whole island could satisfy; and which having, in the reign of James I. and at the Restoration, despoiled the natives of no less than ten millions six hundred and thirty-six thousand eight hundred and thirty-seven acres, now added to its plunder one million sixty thousand seven hundred and ninety-two acres more, being the amount altogether (according to Lord Clare's calculation) of the whole superficial contents of the island!

"Thus, not only had *all* Ireland suffered confiscation in the course of this century, but no inconsiderable portion of it had been twice and even thrice confiscated. Well might Lord Clare say, 'that the situation of the Irish nation, at the Revolution, stands unparalleled in the history of the inhabited world.'" (pp. 111—113.)

By the Articles of Limerick, the Irish were promised the free exercise of their religion; but from that period to the year 1788, every year produced some fresh penalty against that religion, some liberty was abridged, some right impaired, or some suffering in-

creased. By acts in King William's reign, they were
prevented from being solicitors. No Catholic was
allowed to marry a Protestant; and any Catholic who
sent a son to Catholic countries for education was to
forfeit all his lands. In the reign of Queen Anne, any
son of a Catholic who chose to turn Protestant got
possession of the father's estate. No Papist was
allowed to purchase freehold property, or to take a
lease for more than thirty years. If a Protestant dies
intestate, the estate is to go to the next *Protestant* heir,
though all to the tenth generation should be Catholic.
In the same manner, if a Catholic dies intestate, his
estate is to go to the next Protestant. No Papist is to
dwell in Limerick or Galway. No Papist is to take
an annuity for life. The widow of a Papist turning
Protestant to have a portion of the chattels of deceased
in spite of any will. Every Papist teaching schools to
be presented as a regular Popish convict. Prices of
catching Catholic priests, from 50s. to £10, according
to rank. Papists are to answer all questions respecting
other Papists, or to be committed to jail for twelve
months. No trust to be undertaken for Papists. No
Papist to be on Grand Juries. Some notion may be
formed of the spirit of those times, from an order of
the House of Commons, "that the Sergeant-at-Arms
should take into custody all Papists that should presume to come into *the gallery !*" (*Commons' Journal*,
vol. iii., fol. 976.) During this reign the English
Parliament legislated as absolutely for Ireland as they
do now for Rutlandshire, an evil not to be complained
of, if they had done it as justly. In the reign of

George I., the horses of Papists were seized for the
militia, and rode by Protestants; towards which the
Catholics paid double, and were compelled to find
Protestant substitutes.   They were prohibited from
voting at vestries, or being high or petty constables.
An act of the English Parliament in this reign opens
as follows :—" Whereas attempts have been lately
made to shake off the subjection of Ireland to the
Imperial Crown of these realms, be it enacted," etc.
etc.   In the reign of George II. four-sixths of the
population were cut off from the right of voting at
elections by the necessity under which they were
placed of taking the oath of supremacy.   Barristers
and solicitors marrying Catholics are exposed to all
the penalties of Catholics.   Persons robbed by privateers during a war with a Catholic State are to be in-
demnified by a levy on the Catholic inhabitants of the
neighbourhood.   All marriages between Catholics and
Protestants are annulled.   All Popish priests celebrating them are to be hanged.   " This system " (says
Arthur Young) "has no other tendency than that of
driving out of the kingdom all the personal wealth of
the Catholics, and extinguishing their industry within
it; and the face of the country, every object which presents itself to travellers, tells him how effectually this
has been done."—*Young's Tour in Ireland*, vol. ii., p. 48.

Such is the history of Ireland—for we are now at
our own times ; and the only remaining question is,
whether the system of improvement and conciliation
begun in the reign of George III. shall be pursued,

and the remaining incapacities of the Catholics removed, or all these concessions be made insignificant
by an adherence to that spirit of proscription which
they professed to abolish? Looking to the sense and
reason of the thing, and to the ordinary working of
humanity and justice, when assisted, as they are here,
by self-interest and worldly policy, it might seem
absurd to doubt of the result. But looking to the
facts and the persons by which we are now surrounded,
we are constrained to say that we greatly fear that
these incapacities never will be removed till they are
removed by fear. What else, indeed, can we expect
when we see them opposed by such enlightened men as
Mr. Peel—faintly assisted by men of such admirable
genius as Mr. Canning—when Royal Dukes consider
it as a compliment to the memory of their father to
continue this miserable system of bigotry and exclusion,
when men act ignominiously and contemptibly on this
question, who do so on no other question, when almost
the only persons zealously opposed to this general baseness and fatuity are a few Whigs and Reviewers, or
here and there a virtuous poet like Mr. Moore? We
repeat again, that the measure never will be effected
but by fear. In the midst of one of our just and
necessary wars, the Irish Catholics will compel this
country to grant them a great deal more than they at
present require or even contemplate. We regret most
severely the protraction of the disease, and the danger
of the remedy; but in this way it is that human affairs
are carried on!

We are sorry we have nothing for which to praise

Administration on the subject of the Catholic question, but it is but justice to say, that they have been very zealous and active in detecting fiscal abuses in Ireland, in improving mercantile regulations, and in detecting Irish jobs. The commission on which Mr. Wallace presided has been of the greatest possible utility, and does infinite credit to the Government. The name of Mr. Wallace in any commission has now become a pledge to the public that there is a real intention to investigate and correct abuse. He stands in the singular predicament of being equally trusted by the rulers and the ruled. It is a new era in Government when such men are called into action; and if there were not proclaimed and fatal limits to that ministerial liberality, which, so far as it goes, we welcome without a grudge and praise without a sneer, we might yet hope that, for the sake of mere consistency, they might be led to falsify our forebodings. But alas! there are motives more immediate, and therefore irresistible; and the time is not yet come when it will be believed easier to govern Ireland by the love of the many than by the power of the few, when the paltry and dangerous machinery of bigoted faction and prostituted patronage may be dispensed with, and the vessel of the State be propelled by the natural current of popular interests and the breath of popular applause. In the meantime, we cannot resist the temptation of gracing our conclusion with the following beautiful passage, in which the author alludes to the hopes that were raised at another great era of partial concession and liberality, that of the revolution of 1782, when,

also, benefits were conferred which proved abortive
because they were incomplete, and balm poured into
the wound, where the envenomed shaft was yet left to
rankle.

" And here," says the gallant Captain Rock, " as the
free confession of weakness constitutes the chief charm
and use of biography, I will candidly own that the
dawn of prosperity and concord which I now saw
breaking over the fortunes of my country, so dazzled
and deceived my youthful eyes, and so unsettled every
hereditary notion of what I owed to my name and
family, that—shall I confess it—I even hailed with pleasure the prospects of peace and freedom that seemed
opening around me; nay, was ready, in the boyish
enthusiasm of the moment, to sacrifice all my own
personal interest in all future riots and rebellions to
the one bright, seducing object of my country's liberty
and repose.

" When I contemplated such a man as the venerable
Charlemont, whose nobility was to the people like a
fort over a valley, elevated above them solely for their
defence ; who introduced the polish of the courtier
into the camp of the freeman, and served his country
with all that pure Platonic devotion which a true
knight in the time of chivalry proffered to his mistress;
when I listened to the eloquence of Grattan, the very
music of freedom, her first fresh matin song, after a
long night of slavery, degradation, and sorrow ; when
I saw the bright offerings which he brought to the
shrine of his country—wisdom, genius, courage, and

patience, invigorated and embellished by all those
social and domestic virtues, without which the loftiest
talents stand isolated in the moral waste around them,
like the pillars of Palmyra towering in a wilderness!—
when I reflected on all this, it not only disheartened
me for the mission of discord which I had undertaken,
but made me secretly hope that it might be rendered
unnecessary ; and that a country which could produce
such men and achieve such a revolution, might yet—in
spite of the joint efforts of the Government and my
family—take her rank in the scale of nations, and be
happy !

"My father, however, who saw the momentary
dazzle by which I was affected, soon drew me out of
this false light of hope in which I lay basking, and
set the truth before me in a way but too convincing
and ominous. 'Be not deceived, boy,' he would say,
'by the fallacious appearances before you. Eminently
great and good as is the man to whom Ireland owes
this short era of glory, *our* work, believe me, will last
longer than his. We have a power on our side that
"will not willingly let us die;" and, long after
Grattan shall have disappeared from earth like that
arrow shot into the clouds by Alcestes, effecting
nothing, but leaving a long train of light behind him,
the family of the ROCKS will continue to flourish in
all their native glory, upheld by the ever-watchful
care of the Legislature, and fostered by that "nursing-
mother of Liberty," the Church.'"

Printed by Cassell & Company, Limited, La Belle Sauvage, London, E.C.
30.1092

Cassell & Company's Publications.

Educational and Students' Manuals.

Agricultural Text-Books, Cassell's. (The "Downton" Series.) Edited by JOHN WRIGHTSON, Professor of Agriculture. Fully Illustrated, 2s. 6d. each.

- **Farm Crops.** By Prof. WRIGHTSON.
  Soils and Manures. By J. M. H. MUNRO, D.Sc. (London), F.I.C., F.C.S.
  Live Stock. By Prof. WRIGHTSON.

Alphabet, Cassell's Pictorial. 3s. 6d.

Arithmetics, The Modern School. By GEORGE RICKS, B.Sc. Lond. With Test Cards. (*List on application.*)

Atlas, Cassell's Popular. Containing 24 Coloured Maps. 2s. 6d.

Book-Keeping. By THEODORE JONES. For Schools, 2s. ; cloth, 3s. For the Million, 2s. ; cloth, 3s. Books for Jones's System, 2s.

Chemistry, The Public School. By J. H. ANDERSON, M.A. 2s. 6d.

Classical Texts for Schools, Cassell's. (*A List post free on application.*

Cookery for Schools. By LIZZIE HERITAGE. 6d.

Copy-Books, Cassell's Graduated. *Eighteen Books.* 2d. each.

Copy-Books, The Modern School. *Twelve Books.* 2d. each.

Drawing Copies, Cassell's Modern School Freehand. First Grade, 1s. ; Second Grade, 2s.

Drawing Copies, Cassell's " New Standard." *Complete in Fourteen Books.* 2d., 3d., and 4d. each.

N.I.,—E.   1   2.93

Dulce Domum. Rhymes and Songs for Children. Edited by JOHN FARMER. Crown 4to (Old Notation and Words), 5s. ; crown 8vo, in Two Parts (Tonic Sol Fa and Old Notation, and Words), 6d. each.

Energy and Motion. By WILLIAM PAICE, M.A. Illustrated. 1s. 6d.

Euclid, Cassell's. Edited by Prof. WALLACE, M.A. 1s.

Euclid, The First Four Books of. *New Edition.* In paper, 6d. ; cloth, 9d.

Experimental Geometry. By PAUL BERT. Illustrated. 1s. 6d.

French, Cassell's Lessons in. *New and Revised Edition.* Parts I. and II., each 2s. 6d. ; complete, 4s. 6d. Key, 1s. 6d.

French-English and English-French Dictionary. *Entirely New · and Enlarged Edition.* 1,150 pages, 8vo, cloth, 3s. 6d.

French Reader, Cassell's Public School. By G. S. CONRAD. 2s. 6d.

Gaudeamus. Songs for Colleges and Schools. Edited by JOHN FARMER. 5s. Words only, paper covers, 6d. ; cloth, 9d.

German Dictionary, Cassell's New (German-English, English-German). *Cheap Edition.* Cloth, 3s. 6d.

Hand-and-Eye Training. By G. RICKS, B.Sc. 2 Vols., with 16 Coloured Plates in each Vol. Cr. 4to, 6s. each. Cards for Class Use, 5 sets, 1s. each.

Historical Cartoons, Cassell's Coloured. Size 45 in. × 35 in., 2s. each. Mounted on canvas and varnished, with rollers, 5s. each.

Historical Course for Schools, Cassell's. Illustrated throughout.

    I.—Stories from English History, 1s.

    II.—The Simple Outline of English History, 1s. 3d.

    III.—The Class History of England, 2s. 6d.

Latin Dictionary, Cassell's New (Latin - English and English-Latin). Revised by J. R. V. MARCHANT, M.A., and J. F. CHARLES, B.A. Cloth, 3s. 6d.

Latin Primer, The First. By Prof. POSTGATE. 1s.

Latin Primer, The New. By Prof. J. P. POSTGATE. Crown 8vo, 2s. 6d.

Latin Prose for Lower Forms. By M. A. BAYFIELD, M.A. 2s. 6d.

Laundry Work (How to Teach It). By Mrs. E. LORD. 6d.

Laws of Every-Day Life. By H. O. ARNOLD-FORSTER, M.P. 1s. 6d. *Special Edition* on Green Paper for Persons with Weak Eyesight. 2s.

Little Folks' History of England. Illustrated. 1s. 6d.

Making of the Home, The. By Mrs. SAMUEL A. BARNETT. 1s. 6d.

Map-Building Series, Cassell's. Outline Maps prepared by H. O. ARNOLD-FORSTER, M.P. Per Set of Twelve, 1s.

Marlborough Books :—Arithmetic Examples, 3s. Arithmetic Rules, 1s. 6d. French Exercises, 3s. 6d. French Grammar, 2s. 6d. German do., 3s. 6d.

Mechanics for Young Beginners, A First Book of. By the Rev. J. G. EASTON, M.A. 4s. 6d.

Mechanics and Machine Design, Numerical Examples in Practical. By R. G. BLAINE, M.E. With Diagrams. Cloth, 2s. 6d.

Natural History Coloured Wall Sheets, Cassell's New. 18 Subjects. Size 39 by 31 in. Mounted on rollers and varnished. 3s. each.

Object Lessons from Nature. By Prof. L. C. MIALL, F.L.S. *New and Enlarged Edition.* In 2 Vols., 1s. 6d. each.

Perspective, The Principles of. By G. TROBRIDGE. Illustrated. Paper, 1s. 6d. ; cloth, 2s. 6d.

Physiology for Students, Elementary. By A. T. SCHOFIELD, M.D., M.R.C.S., &c. Illustrated. 7s. 6d.

Physiology for Schools. By A. T. SCHOFIELD, M.D., M.R.C.S., &c. Illustrated. Cloth, 1s. 9d. ; Three Parts, paper covers, 5d. each ; or cloth limp, 6d. each.

Poetry Readers, Cassell's New. Illustrated. 12 Books, 1d. each ; or complete in one Vol., cloth, 1s. 6d.

Popular Educator, Cassell's NEW. With Revised Text, New Maps, New Coloured Plates, New Type, &c. In 8 Vols., 5s. each ; or in Four Vols., half-morocco, 50s. the set.

Readers, Cassell's " Higher Class." (*List on application.*)

Readers, Cassell's Readable. Illustrated. (*List on application.*)

Readers for Infant Schools, Coloured. Three Books. 4d. each.

Reader, The Citizen. By H. O. ARNOLD-FORSTER, M.P. Illustrated. 1s. 6d. Also a *Scottish Edition*, cloth, 1s. 6d.

Reader, The Temperance. By Rev. J. DENNIS HIRD. Cr. 8vo, 1s. 6d.

Readers, The " Modern School " Geographical. (*List on application.*)

Readers, The " Modern School." Illustrated. (*List on application.*)

Reckoning, Howard's Anglo-American Art of. By C. FRUSHER HOWARD. Paper covers, 1s. ; cloth, 2s. *New Edition*, 5s.

Round the Empire. By G. R. PARKIN. Fully Illustrated. 1s. 6d.

Science Applied to Work. By J. A. BOWER. 1s.

3

Science of Everyday Life. By J. A. Bower. Illustrated. 1s.

Shade from Models, Common Objects, and Casts of Ornament, How to. By W. E. Sparkes. With 25 Plates by the Author. 3s.

Shakspere's Plays for School Use. 5 Books. Illustrated. 6d. each.

Spelling, A Complete Manual of. By J. D. Morell, LL.D. 1s.

Technical Manuals, Cassell's. Illustrated throughout:—
Handrailing and Staircasing, 3s. 6d.—Bricklayers, Drawing for, 3s.—Building Construction, 2s. — Cabinet-Makers, Drawing for, 3s. — Carpenters and Joiners, Drawing for, 3s. 6d. —Gothic Stonework, 3s.—Linear Drawing and Practical Geometry, 2s.—Linear Drawing and Projection.—The Two Vols. in One, 3s. 6d.—Machinists and Engineers, Drawing for, 4s. 6d.—Metal-Plate Workers, Drawing for, 3s.—Model Drawing, 3s.—Orthographical and Isometrical Projection, 2s.—Practical Perspective, 3s.—Stonemasons, Drawing for, 3s.—Applied Mechanics, by Sir R. S. Ball, LL.D., 2s.—Systematic Drawing and Shading, 2s.

Technical Educator, Cassell's. *Revised Edition.* Four Vols. 5s. each.

Technology, Manuals of. Edited by Prof. Ayrton, F.R.S., and Richard Wormell, D.Sc., M.A. Illustrated throughout :—
The Dyeing of Textile Fabrics, by Prof. Hummel, 5s.—Watch and Clock Making, by D. Glasgow, Vice-President of the British Horological Institute, 4s. 6d.—Steel and Iron, by Prof. W. H. Greenwood, F.C.S., M.I.C.E., &c., 5s.—Spinning Woollen and Worsted, by W. S. B. McLaren, M.P., 4s. 6d.—Design in Textile Fabrics, by T. R. Ashenhurst, 4s. 6d.—Practical Mechanics, by Prof. Perry, M.E., 3s. 6d.—Cutting Tools Worked by Hand and Machine, by Prof. Smith, 3s. 6d.

Things New and Old ; or, Stories from English History. By H. O. Arnold-Forster, M.P. Fully Illustrated. Strongly bound in Cloth. Standards I. & II., 9d. each; Standard III., 1s. ; Standard IV., 1s. 3d. ; Standards V., VI., & VII., 1s. 6d. each.

This World of Ours. By H. O. Arnold-Forster, M.P. Illustrated. 3s. 6d.

CASSELL'S CLASSIFIED CATALOGUE,
containing particulars of upwards of One Thousand Volumes, ranging in price from

THREEPENCE TO FIFTY GUINEAS,

will be sent post free to any address.

CASSELL & COMPANY, Limited, *Ludgate Hill, London.*